I0819906

OUTLAW

The Story of Joe Flick

By the same author:

HarperCollins Publishers Australia

Rotten Gods
Savage Tide
Lethal Sky
Voodoo Dawn (short fiction)

Stories of Oz Publishing

The Hammer of Ramenskoye (short fiction)
Camp Leichhardt
Galloping Jones and Other True Stories from Australia's History
Whistler's Bones
Red Jack and the Ragged Thirteen

OUTLAW

The Story of Joe Flick

Greg Barron

- STORIES OF OZ PUBLISHING -

First edition published 2020
by Stories of Oz Publishing
PO Box K57
Haymarket NSW 1240

ABN: 0920230558
facebook.com/storiesofoz
ozbookstore.com

ISBN: 9780648733812
Proof reading/editing: Robert Barron
and Catriona Martin
Cover design: James Barron based on an
original watercolour by Yvonne Bauer
Typeset in Bembo and Bookman Old Style
Printed and bound in Australia by IngramSpark

The commissioner has wired to Inspector Douglas to go out with any available men, and capture the desperado at all hazards.

QUEENSLAND TIMES OCTOBER 31 1889

TO THE READER

This book is based on a blend of verifiable facts, yarns of varying reliability, and newspaper articles. Where the facts are thin I've used fiction to fill in the gaps and breathe life into the story. There are dozens of versions of Joe Flick's story, and I have tried to go with the most trustworthy aspects of these.

I'd like to thank Dick Eussen, Bob Forsyth, and Costas Constantinides, all enthusiastic researchers into Gulf Country history. Thanks to Don Douglas also, who knows bush and station lore and life so well.

Thanks to my wife Catriona for her love and support, my sons Daly and James and my father Bob who works so hard as a one-man warehousing and distribution network.

Finally to the readers of my stories, I'm forever grateful that you think that they are worth your time.

Greg Barron

February 2020

· CHAPTER 1 ·

Old Doomadgee

IN 1934 I, ROBERT Morris of Burwood, applied to the School of Anthropology, Sydney University, to undertake field research for my doctoral thesis. My father's cousin was a member of the Waitara branch of the Christian Brethren, and through them I was invited to 'visit and assist' at Doomadgee Mission, in the Gulf of Carpentaria. Whilst there I would compile a dictionary of the languages spoken by the Gangalidda and Waanyi people.

Being just twenty-two years old, six-feet-tall but lanky and 'short on common sense,' as my father used to say, my mother was rightly worried at my chances of reaching my destination, let alone surviving six months in the wild Gulf. Even so, with her tears still damp on my shirt, I steered my four-cylinder Riley motor-car out of our depression-ravaged suburb, north to Newcastle, then onto the New England Highway with the windows wide open and the warm November air on my face.

I'd changed and repaired my first flat tyre before I was through the Hunter Valley, busted an axle in Tingha, and got bogged in the black soils near Moree. I camped each night beside my car, learned to cook on an open fire and make the best of what I had. These skills would stand me in good stead in the sands of North Africa, eight or nine years later, when I carried a Lee Enfield rifle for my country, but that's another story.

This journey north was character building, to say the least. I waited three days for the repair of a front spring in Augathella and swore like a teamster when the petrol tank ran dry five miles short of Longreach. Near Winton I picked up a swagman to keep me company. A hundred miles later, after we had parted company, I discovered that he had emptied my wallet of cash. Luckily I'd followed my father's advice and hidden the bulk of my funds under the dash.

Finally, I reached Burketown, a ghost town in a state of torpor under a broiling heat, with the high, brown Albert River lapping at the edges. There I filled the trunk with provisions for the Mission, and obtained a hand-drawn mud map of the final leg. Two days later; four weeks after my mother's final kiss, the Riley churned through the ruts over a tidal clay pan, and spun her rear wheels up the rise into the old Doomadgee Mission west of Arthur's Creek at Bayley Point.

I looked around me with the eyes of a young man eager for adventure, anxious to learn what my home over the next months would be like. The mission occupied, essentially but not strictly, an island of green, some six miles by two or three in extent, surrounded by marshes and saltwater inlets on all sides. To the north was the Gulf of Carpentaria – of a colour unfamiliar to me – a kind of blue-green-grey. A mangrove-lined creek snaked its way past the Mission lands to the east. Most of the high ground was lightly wooded, and soon enough I would learn to tell a carbeen tree from a messmate, but on that first day they were just trees, and a scrubby type they were too.

The Mission itself, when I reached it, occupied a sandy ridge overlooking more swamps. It was neat, but more primitive than I had expected. All the buildings – a couple of outhouses, and two dormitories, presumably one for boys and one for girls – were made of pandanus-palm logs standing on end, with corrugated tin or speargrass thatch roofs. I noted horse yards, a vegetable garden fenced with wire netting, and the beginnings of an orchard. A woman was carrying a bucket of water up from the well, located on the edge of the marshes.

The Missionaries, Len and Dorothy Akehurst, along with their young son, Frank, met me at the car, bustled me inside their home and had me drinking tea in no time. Len was taller than me, and thin as a whip, but with big hands and a wiry knottiness to his muscles. His corded neck was the same width as his face. Dorothy looked small beside him, with kind eyes and dark curls. They were, all in all, serious but friendly souls. They told me how they had first tried their luck at building a mission in Burketown itself, near the racecourse, but were forced out here, to this genuine wilderness, by the negative attitudes of the local white population.

The Akehursts gave me a private room in one of the outbuildings, with a kapok mattress and bed-base cleverly made of timber branches. The floor was of crushed termite mound, almost as hard as concrete. Most of the furniture, it turned out, had been made by or under the supervision of Bob Gates, a carpenter from Tasmania. He lived in another room in the same dwelling as I, and proved to be good company.

In those first days, fired with academic purpose and the obvious presence of God in this place, I set about my task with energy. I had an indexed notebook for words and their meanings, one for grammar rules and one for phrases. Len and Dorothy provided my first few Waanyi and Ganglalidda words, for they had been doing their best to learn the local tongues when they could. They introduced me to the mission children, who had mostly been brought from Burketown, and who further enlightened me to the secrets of their dialects, making me smile in the process. Meanwhile, the good missionaries dosed me up on quinine to keep the Gulf Fever at bay, and I did not have to raise a hand to feed myself, apart from sometimes indulging in the pleasurable sport of fishing.

In my free time, I was drawn to the country itself. I took rambling walks to the beach, venturing carelessly at times into the sucking mud of the mangroves. I sketched Pains and Bayley Islands, mangrove swamps and stands of pandanus trees. I saw brolgas dance, and morning glory clouds. One day I watched Nichol, one of the Gangalidda workers, whistle up an emu, bewitching it into coming close, at which point he rose and clubbed it to death for the pot.

Over time, I developed relationships with all the pivotal characters in the local scene: Bob Gates and his offsider, Frank: the aforementioned Nichol, young Stanley and his brother Willie. Lizzie and her daughter, Dulcie. There was also Mahomet Hussein, who lived a hermit's life along the coast a little, but idled away much of his time at the mission.

Growing in confidence, and seeking older, more accomplished speakers of the local languages, I also ventured into the camp of itinerants on the eastern side of the 'island,' along the banks of Doomadgee Creek, the western arm of Arthur's Creek. I found that if I took a little tobacco with me, the inhabitants were more amenable to conversation.

I met an old man called Charlie, who knew scarcely a word of English but loved to go to the missionaries' Saturday night prayer meetings, dressed only in a loincloth. I also made the acquaintance of a famous dugong hunter called Old Jack, who still pursued the aquatic beasts with a spear and sixteen-foot dugout. Others sat around smoky fires, with scores of whippet-thin dogs in attendance, these half-starved canines chewing on fish bones and tortoise shells; anything that resembled food.

One particular old woman interested me from the start, for several reasons. One was her age, she looked to be at least eighty years, and her eyes were pale with the effects of sandy blight. The other reason was that the others spoke to her little and she kept her own fire. Her 'white' name, I learned, was Kitty. Her dusty, charcoal-shaded skin was pitted by a multitude of old scars, most notably on her forehead and chest. She sat in the shade through much of the day, usually in her own camp, but sometimes alongside the creek near the jetty, or occasionally venturing up near to the mission buildings.

When I queried Len Akehurst about her, he told me that Kitty was not from this country like the others, her birthplace being outback New South Wales. Learning that she was a fellow New South Welshman piqued my interest still further.

Then came the bombshell. Kitty, Len told me, had been the wife of a white cattleman for more than thirty years, and her long-dead son was an infamous outlaw.

Outlaw? My ears pricked up like those of a rabbit. Being young, and a romantic at heart, I was fascinated by feats of arms and drawn by the nature of my profession to the science of crime.

The next few afternoons I spent sitting in the shade with Kitty. She spoke English better than most of the others in that camp, perhaps because of her years in company with a white man. A clay pipe, scorched around the bowl, sat between her lips or in her hand most of the time; sometimes lit, sometimes not.

Occasionally, tiring of my questions, she would stand up and move. At other times she would accept gifts of tea or tobacco, and let me sit for hours, feigning deafness when I probed too deep.

Day by day, however, I suspected that she was growing to like me. I learned that she preferred Capstan tobacco to Barrett's, and despite her near-blindness she could tell the difference straight off. Her bad vision, it seemed, bothered her little. She could cook, fish, and walk reasonably long distances when necessary.

Kitty had a wicked sense of humour. One day, for example, when we lounged and talked down at the creek, she was sitting with her back against a tree while I sat cross-legged, facing away from the water. At intervals she would chuckle to herself.

'What's so funny?' I asked.

Kitty pointed out at the racing ebb tide and said, 'Big-feller 'gator many time poke him head up an' look at you. Might be he wanna eat you up.' How she noticed this with her poor eye-sight was beyond my comprehension.

That afternoon, as if to reward me for amusing her, she told me a little about her husband, whose name was Henry. Unlike most white stockmen and their women, Kitty told me proudly that she and Henry were 'proper way married.' From a pocket in her dress she produced a grimy pewter ring.

Henry's family were German immigrants, she told me, his father Casper Flecke having been a vine dresser. (If I was surprised that Kitty knew the term, I was even more surprised that she could tell me exactly what work vine dressers did, conjuring imaginary vines and the dresser's secateurs with her hands). This was not the last time she would surprise me. I was to find that her memory for places, people, conversations – incidents that people had described to her – was as sharp as a Kodak print.

She went on to relate how the Flecke family's passage to Australia was paid for by the famous Macarthurs of Sydney, so Casper could work on their vineyards at Camden. After the five-year contract expired the family anglicised their name to Flick and drifted north to Maitland, where Casper became a spirit merchant, and young Henry fell into bush work on outlying stations, drifting further afield as he grew older.

Henry had been working on Mungyer Station, near Moree, when he took Kitty from a camp along the Mehi River.

'He took you?' I asked.

Kitty agreed that yes, he had found her alone, ridden her down and taken her on his horse. Of course she had been terrified. He taught her to ride, wear stockman's clothes and tend cattle. Kitty, in dungarees and shirt, worked beside her man by day, and shared his swag at night.

'From now on,' he said, 'your name is Kitty.'

Three times she repeated her real name.

'Forget that one. Kitty's your name now.'

When Kitty became pregnant she continued to ride beside Henry and work with cattle. Their son, Joe, was born in a stock camp on Mungyer Station.

Henry was enamoured of the child, and declared him to be the best-formed little fellow he had seen.

Our talks were interrupted when the first days of heavy rain came. I now learned why the Mission lands were so often described as an island, for the encircling arms of water joined hands and cut us off. The humidity grew to unbearable levels, so that I sweltered day and night, and Dorothy Akehurst was struck down with fever.

Then, when the sun was shining again, producing a steaming heat that I could scarcely bear, I walked into Kitty's camp with a lump of damper and some tea. That day Kitty started to tell me about Joe. Later I was able to add to her story some details that I researched and learned first-hand from court records, and newspaper archives, for Kitty cared little for dates and times.

In the main, however, what follows is the story she told. I learned that for people who do not write, stories travel from lip to lip with perfect accuracy. And for them, truth can be a matter of life and death. Those parts of Joe's life Kitty had not seen with her own eyes, she had learned from others, and related word-for-word.

Quite early in our talks, she told me that the police shot Joe at least nine times before he fell dead, and I began to understand that few people carried such a burden of pain as that old woman. From that time on, neither heat nor monsoonal downpours could stop my time with Kitty.

Before long, whether toiling away at my thesis, or sweating in my bed, under a net besieged by centipedes and mosquitoes, I was dreaming of Kitty's outlaw son. Dreaming of the way it might have been near the end, with bullet wounds oozing blood from his gut, thigh, chest and limbs, and his lean face like a death's-head in the dusk, and God only knew what police skulking nearby.

I came to understand that Joe Flick, the grandson of a German vine dresser and a Kamilaroi warrior, was the truest wild colonial boy of them all.

I hungered for his story like a starving man.

· CHAPTER 2 ·

The Brook Hotel

At the Mission; that island in the clay and salt of the wild Gulf shore, came days of building heat, followed by thunderstorms such as I had never dreamed possible. Raking winds and black thunderheads roved ahead of a packed, boiling cloud mass, spitting lightning over a shallow sea churned to a furious white.

Years later I would see ranks of German soldiers and their Panzer IV tanks through the blowing sands of El Alamein and feel that same sense of awe and powerlessness. I was learning something that my city upbringing had not taught me; that there are powers in the world far greater than our pitiful selves.

I took to visiting with Kitty in the late mornings, while the Mission children were still at their lessons. So involved in the story was I, that in those days I scarcely touched ink to my notebooks. Len Akehurst lectured me mildly for neglecting my work, but I felt myself bound up with Kitty's story, and could not let go.

When Joe was still an infant, Kitty told me, Henry Flick moved the small family up into Queensland, where he found a job working sheep on Murweh Station. He kept Kitty and their son in a wurlie made of bark and scraps of tin on the waterhole near the homestead, coming home after days out on the run smelling of wool, dust and rum. He was a hard man, with steely blue eyes, and knife-scars on his hand and left thumb, but he loved his little boy.

One morning Henry rode back from a weekend of drinking and gambling in Charleville, and took from his pocket a ring he'd won at cards. He slid it onto Kitty's finger. 'There you go. Now we're prop'ly married.'

This gesture didn't dampen Henry's interest in other women, for around this time at Murweh he became enamoured of a Kunja girl named Lizzie, who worked as a maid at the homestead. He studied her movements – noticing that after supper, when she finished her work, she usually walked alone out to the servant's huts.

The following night, with Kitty and Joe packed up and waiting, Henry rode up to the homestead, hid behind a bush with a spare horse, and waited for the girl to come. He clamped a hand over her mouth and carried her away. With a good moon, he, Kitty, little Joe and Lizzie were soon on their way to the Bulloo River.

Jenkins, the station owner, was furious at the loss. The following morning he, his eldest son and a tracker set off in pursuit of their missing housemaid. Henry, however, was expecting them. Twenty miles down the track, he sent Kitty, Joe, and Lizzie on ahead, and waited behind a convenient outcrop.

When the riders came up, Henry appeared with a double-barrelled gun in his hands, and a hatchet in his belt. 'Go home you bastards,' he said, addressing Jenkins and his son. 'I've got one cartridge for each of you, and an axe for whatever's left.'

Jenkins and his son spat and swore, but turned their mounts for home. That, however, wasn't the end of the matter. The police were soon in pursuit, and Joe was four years old when he watched uniformed men knock his father from his horse with rifle butts, then force him to kneel and wear chains. In that state they dragged Henry Flick, with his family following miserably behind, to Charleville, where he was charged with aggravated assault and sentenced to six months in Roma gaol. Lizzie was returned to the Jenkins family.

Kitty was not judged to be a fit carer for her son without Henry, so Joe was made to stay with a succession of police families, while his mother made camp by the river and waited, pining for her son, starving herself until her legs were like sticks and the townspeople fed her out of pity.

Despite publicly swearing that he would 'scalp' the entire Jenkins family for calling the traps on him, Henry left the district as soon as he was released. Feeling increasingly like outcasts, the little family rode north on 'borrowed' horses for the Gulf, where a score of new stations needed good stockmen – and Henry was handy with horses, sheep and cattle – resilient and self-reliant.

Moving ever northward, packhorses carried everything the family owned to Lawn Hill station.

There, for the first time, they saw the homestead and its steep descent to the creek where much later Joe would make his last bloody stand. This picturesque pandanus and paperbark lined waterway, with its dramatic ochre-hued cliffs had seemed, back then, like a land of promise.

Lawn Hill Station had several absentee shareholders, but Frank Hann was the man on the spot, owner and manager all-in-one. Born in Dorsetshire, England, and immigrating while still a child, Frank Hann's feats of exploration and endurance were well known and celebrated amongst his peers.

In 1872, he and his brother William, along with a botanist, a geologist and others, travelled north on a Queensland Government sponsored expedition to investigate the country 'North to the 14th Parallel'. Rugged country even now, in those days Cape York was an area even the toughest settlers and adventurers avoided.

Hann located a river beginning in the hills west of Port Douglas, flowing westwards for six-hundred-kilometres before it emptied into the Mitchell River, ultimately reaching the Gulf of Carpentaria. He named this waterway the Palmer River after the Chief Secretary of Queensland, Arthur Palmer. Hann and his comrades were the first to pan gold from the river in 1872. The amounts were not significant, but enough to begin the wild Palmer River gold rush.

Frank was not big or robust, as might be expected of a man with his reputation. Rather, he was more bird than bull, with red bushy eyebrows and flaming hair. He lived openly with not one, but several black concubines (I can think of no better word), though his white mates accepted the pretence that these women were housemaids.

Hann signed Henry up on the spot, and offered him a place to camp near the homestead.

Within a year or two, Kitty told me proudly, Joe was riding his own horse, and could crack a stock whip like a man. By eight years of age he could drop a running wallaby with one shot at a hundred yards, and dress it in a blink.

Frank Hann had been aware of deposits of silver ore, in the form of galena, on the station for some time, and when he started work on extraction, he drafted Henry into the enterprise.

With Joe's father now officially a miner, life changed. The days of travelling were over, and the new camp near the mine became a home. Father and son built a couple of stout huts, and the small family put down roots. It was a busy, friendly camp, with a couple of labourers, raised from the local Waanyi, thrown in. Henry brought other women into his bed, when they took his fancy, but Kitty was too intent on the survival of herself and her son to indulge in jealousy.

She toiled from sun-up onwards, and in the heat of the day, she sat in the shade and plaited cabbage-tree hats to sell to stockmen and travellers. Most days, she was happy enough if Henry did not smack the side of her face and leave it stinging, or throw a rum-angry fist into her stomach or eye.

By the age of thirteen, Joe had roamed every inch of the surrounding wilderness, learning bushcraft from the Waanyi. Before long he was supplementing the family income with stock work on Lawn Hill and other nearby stations such as Punjaub and Westmoreland. The family boosted their store-bought rations with bronzed barramundi and catfish from the creeks, and the occasional 'lost' bullock.

Joe could whistle so beautifully it would make you cry, and stun a goanna at fifty yards with a stone. He had a smile that won over men and women alike. He grew to manhood in this way, close to both his parents, and as fine a bushman as any man alive. He was part horse, part bush spirit, Henry used to say. Neither tobacco nor drink tempted him, and he did a man's work well in every role he cared to fill, always with a flashing smile and good grace.

This was the first time, since I'd arrived at Doomadgee Mission, that I saw Kitty truly smile. It was like she'd forgotten I was there. Her translucent eyes looked skyward, and her toothless lips cracked open.

'Sounds like your son was something special,' I said.

Kitty closed her eyes and nodded thoughtfully.

Joe was twenty-one years old, when the day came that changed it all.

'Hey Joey, we got no sugar,' Henry growled one morning, head and shoulders into the tucker-box that held their supplies.

'Not more than a cupful,' Joe agreed.

'Not much tea neither.'

'Scarcely a week, I reckon.'

Henry Flick turned a liquor bottle upside down and nary a drop appeared.

'Looks like a trip to Burketown, son. Take your mama with you to tail the horses.'

Joe strapped his revolver belt on, and whistled up the packs. They were on the road before the sun had peered over the red stone ridges around the mine. Joe had another reason to look forward to the trip. There was a young housemaid at the Brook, and they had held hands last time he had seen her.

And didn't mother and son love to ride together! Laughing, speaking a mix of English, Kriol, and her native Kamilaroi from down south, they crossed to the Gregory River along a dry scrub of bloodwood and termite mounds, an area that had come to be known as Kitty's Plains.

The Gregory was still full from the Wet, the pandanus roots submerged, and the water retreating, leaving green couch-grass spidering on the banks. Striped archer fish patrolled the shallows, and rainbow bee-eaters flicked low over the surface. Kitty and Joe saw the first dragonflies that day, and knew that the season's change was coming.

Later, riding along the high western bank of the river, Kitty spotted a tell-tale hole high up in an ironwood tree, with a file of stingless bees emerging. She climbed the trunk like a possum, shimmying up with a hatchet, chopping into the hard wood with practiced strokes, then wrapping chunks of sweet sugar-bag honey in paperbark sheets. Mother and son ate the sweet syrup and dried meat by the fire that night, then amused each other by mimicking the creatures of the bush, and Kitty told stories from her inexhaustible supply.

Just before they reached the small settlement at Beame's Brook, Joe's gelding, newly broken, was squeezed against a tree by Kitty's mount and he lashed out with his back legs. His aim was bad, and his near hoof struck the woman's shin. Within an hour the limb was swollen red, blue and painful. It seemed best that she should wait and rest the injury while Joe went on to Burketown.

Joe made a camp for his mother along the creek where she could sit and fish, then went to the Brook Hotel – a solid affair of split logs and weatherboard. Jim Cashman, the owner, was behind the bar. His young wife Mary sat on a chair at the nearest table, an infant girl on her lap against her rounded belly.

'Well if it isn't Yella Joe,' Cashman said. He was originally from Sydney, but had made his name and modest fortune looking out for the main chance in North Queensland. A well-known businessman on the Palmer Fields, he had moved on after the death of his first wife, Margaret, in Cooktown.

'Where's your old man?' Cashman asked.

'Back home. I've left Mama down the creek with a crook leg, I didn't want to take her down to the black's camp while I go into Burketown. Will you keep an eye on her?'

'Course I will, Joey. She'll be safe here.'

'Can I see Ellen for a minute?'

'No, you can't Joe, she's busy making up rooms right now. Now go on, off you go like a good boy. Maybe next time.'

While Joe pushed on with the packs, Kitty sat, fished on the bank, using grasshoppers and flies for bait, and waited. The next day a man from the camp came down to the river to water his horse. He was heavy in the gut, and his teeth rotten from too much sugar.

Kitty recognised him as a slave-boy belonging to Jim Cashman.

The intruder stared at Kitty, but said nothing.

Later on, in the afternoon, he returned. Kitty hid when she heard him coming, but he found her, knocked her down, examined her face up close, then looped a noose around her neck and dragged her to his camp.

On the way they passed the pub, and Cashman himself was standing out the front.

'Hey, boy, you know that's Henry Flick's woman?'

'She's mine now, boss.'

'I don't recommend crossing Flick, but that's your look out.'

At the camp Kitty's new 'husband' told her to cook him up some tucker and she had no choice but to obey. Later on, when the meal was finished, he raped her.

Meanwhile Joe hurried the thirty miles to Burketown, where his senses reeled with the tidal smells of the Albert River. Not far from town he ran into a mate, Monaghan Wilson by name, who also had a white father and Aboriginal mother. He and another man, William Haynes, had stolen a brace of horses from the Gaynor run downriver, and Monaghan was holding the plant while Haynes rode in for rations.

'Come with us, Joe,' smiled Monaghan over a pannikin of black tea. 'We'll sell this lot in Croydon and have a spree.'

'Not this time mate,' said Joe. 'I've plenty of paid work lined up as soon as the season starts.'

After an hour or two of pleasant talk, he rode on from the scrub, and into the broad streets of Burketown.

Only a few dozen whites lived permanently in the town, though seamen from regular shipping traffic, and passing droving teams, helped support the two pubs.

Most of the inhabitants treated Joey with tolerant politeness. They called him Yella Joe, but took him seriously. After all, he dressed like a white man, talked like one, and could out-ride and out-shoot most of them.

Burketown had two stores, one owned by the Watson brothers, and the other by Burns, Philp and Company. Competition between the two outfits was such that discounts could be had.

Joe worked through the shopping list in his head, and finally, with pack-saddles bulging, he rode back to the Brook in high spirits, passing a couple of Afghans and their camel trains along the way. He was stunned to find his mother's camp abandoned, still with some of her things littered on the ground.

Guessing what might have happened, he picked up her belongings, then rode through the riverside camps until he found Kitty at the fire of Cashman's slave-boy, her captor sitting at the entrance of his wurlie, grinning like a king and fingering a long knife.

When Joe pulled up his horse, dismounted, and met his mother's eye, something like a Gulf-country storm grew inside him. And as Kitty described that moment I could feel every heartbeat, even then, forty-five years later.

· CHAPTER 3 ·

The 'Shooting' of Cashman

CASHMAN'S BOY SAW JOE coming, and rose to his full height, brandishing the knife. 'You been lookout for trouble with me?' he asked.

He hadn't reckoned on the way Joe covered the ground between them, scarcely having time to raise his guard before copping a right-cross flush to his jaw. Joe was not a big man – five feet eight or nine – but his hands were over-sized, hard from work, and he was lightning quick.

Henry had taught Joe the basics. The rest he'd worked out for himself. The other man's knife swung on empty space, then fell to the ground from an arm numbed to the shoulder. Joe fought with instinctive grace, whip-like speed and savage power.

The one-sided fight attracted a crowd, and in the end three men were needed to drag Joe from his victim, now a pitiful sight, holding a broken jaw and wailing, his face slick with blood. One of his trouser cuffs was smoking, and his foot was blistered, from a backwards step into the fire.

Joe stood, chest heaving, while the crowd surged back out of reach. 'That man deserved a beating,' he said, 'and none of you can deny it!'

When he had calmed down, Joe helped his mother to a horse, hating the shame on her face. Shame that had been foisted on her by an act of violent lust.

They rode in silence, heading back to Kitty's camp for her things. Then, Joe's anger still undampened, he bathed his face in the river, dabbing the cool liquid where a few despairing blows had landed. Watching the insects swirling in the sunlight around the pandanus, tears pricked his eyes at the thought of what had happened.

'I shouldn't have left you,' he said.

'It's not your fault,' said Kitty. 'It was him – a bad man – who took me, and Cashman saw him drag me along his camp. He could have stopped it.'

'Cashman saw him take you?'

Kitty nodded fearfully.

Joe helped her into the saddle, and sent her home, with the pack horses on a string. 'Go ahead now,' he told her. 'I'll follow along directly.'

'Don't do anything you can't take back,' Kitty warned, but once she had gone, Joe mounted up, and urged his gelding up to the pub. Riding up to the front verandah, he saw Jim Cashman, red faced and furious, standing in the doorway.

'How dare you lay a hand on my boy,' Cashman shouted. 'You've broken his jaw. I'll see you arrested, Yella Joe.'

But Joe's temper was flickering and rumbling, building power and menace. 'You let him take my Mama, you saw him do it. She told me.'

'I don't interfere with your lot,' retorted the pub owner. 'There's no profit in doing so, and you know it. Now make yourself scarce or I'll have you charged with assault. Damned half-breed.'

Joe was about to spur his horse and follow his mother, but this last insult broke something inside him. Without stopping to think he did something that changed his life. Shortened his life. Made him a wanted man.

Taking out his revolver, and waving it with a flourish, he fired a shot into the wall just above the door where Cashman was standing. For a 'boy' such as Joe to fire on a white man was bad enough, but Mary Cashman, without Joe's knowledge, had walked up behind her husband and copped a face full of wood splinters and dust, causing her to cry out and fall.

Joe saw the woman go down. Believing that he had accidentally shot her, he applied his spurs to the gelding and galloped away in a panic. He had never come up against the law in his life, and apart from a few 'dodged' cattle he had not given them reason. That fact, he now knew, had changed.

Kitty reined in some five miles up the track, watching anxiously for Joe. Her bruised leg had mostly healed, but riding was causing her some pain, so resting while she waited seemed like the best course of action.

Before long, she heard urgent hoofbeats. Her relief at seeing Joe changed to alarm as she saw the troubled expression on his face.

'I've maybe shot Mrs Cashman. I don't know,' he said, reining in beside her.

Kitty's first reaction was a pitiful wail. Finally she managed, 'How?'

'I fired a shot. I just wanted to scare Cashman. I didn't know that she was standing behind him.'

Neither of them could think of any plan better than to keep heading for home, though Kitty wept a little as they rode. Both were skilled riders, and their pace was limited only by the packs. Continuing long into the night, Kitty ignoring the nuisance pain in her leg, they stopped only to water the horses, finally reaching their camp around midnight.

Henry came out from the hut to meet them. 'Strange time to be getting home,' he said. 'What's happened?'

Joe dismounted, and while they unloaded the supplies, he told his father everything. 'I lost my temper,' he explained.

Henry covered his face with his hands. His reaction seemed to emphasise the gravity of the situation. 'You were right to punish the man who hurt your mother, and you saved me the trouble of wreaking havoc on him myself.'

'But I might have shot Missus Cashman.'

'Pah,' said Henry. 'One thing I know about you, Joey, is that you hit what you aim at. Besides, that damned Mary Kearney ... she was nothing but a housemaid until she got her hooks into Jim, and every man-jack knows that she's a one-woman melodrama into the bargain.' Henry packed and lit his pipe, deep in thought. 'If you run, Joey, they'll hunt you down. You have to ride into Burketown and give yourself up.'

Kitty was shaking her head from side to side, keening softly. 'No, no, no.'

'It's the best thing to do,' Henry insisted. 'My guess is that Mary won't be hurt too bad, and Joey will get only a light sentence.'

None of them slept that night, but sat around the fire, watching the deep orange coals spit and spark, talking of horses and the bush, and the constellations of stars that sprawled across the heavens above the red earth and rock that surrounded them.

In those hours of waiting Joe thought deeply about what had happened at Beames Brook. After more than twenty years of living with Henry Flick, the cheap ring on Kitty's finger did not fool anybody. She was not Henry's wife. To the world out there she was just Henry's gin. She was property, and property could be stolen and used. Likewise, Henry felt himself free to take other women, sometimes living with them for months on end.

Joe was glad, then, that he had stood up for his mother, whatever the consequences, and vowed that he would go on doing so. The system, he realised, was weighted against those caught in the twilight of one world and the dawn of another.

In the first flush of daylight, Joe said goodbye to his father. Placing his arm around his mother's shoulders, he kissed her tearful cheeks, then saddled and bridled a fresh horse. He was about to ride off, when Henry walked up and plucked Joe's revolver from its holster.

'No guns, son. For all our sakes, just give yourself up and take what they dish out.'

Joe agreed, but he hated riding off into a now-hostile land without a weapon.

The German vine-dresser's son was far from perfect, but he loved his boy.

After stewing through the early part of the morning, Henry told Kitty to stay at home, saddled his horse and set off for the Brook. Riding hard, he reached the pub just after dark, with the interior lit by slush lanterns, and the drinking just warming up – ringers, prospectors and travellers gripping their frothy glasses – and an Irishman's fiddle caterwauling in a corner.

Ignoring the crowd, Henry walked unarmed but still dangerously into the bar. He was no longer young, but his arms and shoulders were heavy with muscle from long days swinging a hammer or pick at the mine.

Not only was Jim Cashman present, but his wife Mary as well, large as life and seemingly unhurt. She ducked out as soon as she recognised the visitor, though Cashman himself stood his ground, even when Henry walked up as close as the slab bar allowed him to.

'Where's my son?' Henry demanded.

Cashman's right hand delved under the bar, and Henry guessed that he had a weapon there ready. 'On his way to Burketown with Constable Hasenkamp and his trackers. Joe tried to kill me, you know.'

'Like hell he did,' Henry snarled. 'If Joe wanted to kill you you'd be dead. Now tell me, what have they charged him with?'

'I don't know.'

'You do know, for you made the complaint. Tell me.'

Cashman licked his lips, his eyes now furtive. Slowly he raised his hand until the barrel, cylinder and cocked hammer of a Smith and Wesson Model 3 appeared over the bar. 'Get out of here or I'll be within my rights to shoot you dead.'

Henry was not afraid. He slapped the revolver from Cashman's hand, and it clattered to the floor. The fiddle stopped scraping and all conversation ceased. Every eye in that bar was on the confrontation now.

'Tell me, you bastard,' shouted Henry. 'What crime have they charged my boy with?'

'Attempted murder,' said Cashman. 'They've charged the yella bastard with attempted murder.'

Henry's hand stiffened, and his heart seemed to stop beating. He walked outside, where the horses were lined up, tethered to hitching posts, and the drinkers' 'boys' sat talking around small fires nearby.

Henry looked up at the darkened sky, still touched with the last pink shades of sunset.

'Oh God what have I done,' he croaked out. 'I should have let my Joey run.'

· CHAPTER 4 ·

Hasenkamp

WORK AT THE DOOMADGEE Mission continued, despite rain and humid heat. Len Akehurst toiled from before dawn to long after dusk, assisting with building works, teaching lessons, carrying water, performing the occasional baptism and preaching at prayer meetings. He had, during his training, completed a course in basic dentistry, and ringers from nearby stations would sometimes ride in to get a tooth removed, or an abscess drained.

For my own part I found that if I applied myself to my thesis work for an hour or two each morning, my grasp on the local languages grew apace. I also became fond of Dorothy Akehurst, for she understood my interest in the story of Joe Flick. We both felt in our souls the sadness that underpinned the tale. A friend from Brisbane sent her an old newspaper clipping about Joe from one of the city papers – raw sensationalism it seemed to me – but I added it to my notes.

Meanwhile, amidst the occasional berthing of the supply boat *Noosa* in the creek, the shenanigans and politics of the camp, and the never-failing delight I took in the chattering, friendly joyfulness of the Mission children, my meetings with Kitty continued.

I learned to wait while she rolled tobacco between her palms, stuffed the bowl of her pipe full and lit it with an ember from the fire. Seeing how badly some parts of Joe's story affected her, this ritual allowed her time to collect herself.

'By and by I'll tell you about that Constable Hasenkamp,' she said to me. 'That p'liceman who arrested Joey.'

'If you want to,' I said.

Kitty took a deep draw on her pipe, watched the stream of smoke she exhaled, then began.

Mounted Constable Harry Hasenkamp was square-jawed, five feet ten in height, broad shoulders tight against his blue serge jacket, and as hard as granite. Like Joe Flick, he was the son of a German immigrant, his father Adolphus then being the pound-keeper down in Ipswich.

Harry Hasenkamp was good mates with Jim Cashman. Their children played together when the publican was in Burketown, and they drank beer shoulder to shoulder at Missus Synott's Commercial Hotel. Both men were shocked that Joe would have had the gall to shoot at a white businessman, no matter what the reason.

Now, riding with two trackers up the Gregory on their way to the Lawn Hill silver mine, Hasenkamp took no chances. He prided himself on never shirking from his duty, but nor did he take unnecessary risks. With his wife, Mary Jane, four daughters and a son back in Burketown, he had no desire to be carried home in a wagon tray.

When the lead tracker spotted Joe heading towards them, along that narrow river trail, Hasenkamp ordered his men to dismount, take cover in the scrub, and train their Martini-Henry carbines on the lone figure as he walked his horse towards them.

'Stop there, Joe Flick,' called Hasenkamp as soon as Joe was within earshot. 'Dismount and kneel.'

Joe had seen men shot for running, so he did as he was told, getting down on one knee, still holding the reins in his right hand. The police surrounded him, forefingers resting on their triggers. One took the reins, another lifted him by the shoulders and patted him down, taking his knife and a couple of cartridges for the revolver he no longer carried, rattling around in the pockets of his dungarees.

'Where are you off to, Joe?' asked Hasenkamp.

Joe said nothing, just raised his arms in a gesture of surrender.

'Smart boy, at least that saves us the trouble of looking for you.'

'Did I kill Mrs Cashman?'

'No, you did not. Though you tried hard enough to kill her husband. You shot nothing but a wall, yet if your aim was better you'd be swinging from a rope inside a week. As it is you'll spend a good deal of your youth learning better manners.'

Joe said nothing. He instinctively understood something about men in authority. That they were friendly as long as he was a good and respectful 'boy', and played the part they expected him to play. He had stepped outside that role and now he must pay the penalty.

Hasenkamp secured Joe with a neck-chain, fastening it with a Yale lock. The cold iron sat hard against his young skin, but the humiliation sat harder still. This treatment didn't seem fair. After all, apart from the man who raped his mother, who deserved a beating, Joe had hurt no one.

The following day, at Burketown Police Station, after a sleepless night camped in irons, and many hard miles on horseback, Joe was formally charged. Hasenkamp wrote words on a page that made the young man legally responsible for the 'Attempted Murder of Patrick James Cashman.'

Joe could not read, but he saw the ink-lines that made up those words winding like snake-trails across the charge-sheet and they chilled him to the bone.

The lock-up was a fortified hut just behind the station, and Joe was too miserable to do anything but sit on the wooden bench inside. He was the only occupant, with the sounds of drunken laughter from the pubs, the occasional cries of curlew and owls, and chattering geckoes for company.

The next morning Constable Hasenkamp, with freshly-shined Napoleon boots and pressed cord breeches, walked Joe to the court house, gripping his arm like a big-game hunter with his kill, for the benefit of the crowd of local business types and loafers who gathered to see Joe face court.

Inside, the magistrate occupied the bench in self-important silence, in his dark suit and bow tie. His name was Alick Clarence Lawson, just thirty years of age. His wife Olympia sat in the third row, looking admiringly up at her husband, while the buttons of her bodice strained with the pressure of her generous proportions.

Alick and Olympia had been married the previous December, in the midst of an Albert River flood, and the wedding party was forced to trudge through a foot of mud and water to attend the ceremony. Reports of the best man, diminutive Lawn Hill Station owner Frank Hann, lifting the eighteen-stone Olympia down from her palanquin outside the National Bank had now passed into local folklore.

Yet, in spite of the local fun-poking at his wife and nuptials, Police Magistrate Lawson was a young man who took himself and his job very seriously. He peered down at Joe solemnly, his bowler hat sitting beside him on the bench.

In near silence Lawson considered the evidence as it was presented: written testaments from witness-es, a scrap of weatherboard complete with embedded slug, formerly a panel from the Brook Hotel, and a matching revolver cartridge from Joe's pockets.

Jim Cashman swept in, freshly shaved and groomed, wearing a morning coat, knee-high riding boots and a safari hat in one hand. He shook hands with Harry Hasenkamp, swore on the Bible to tell the truth and nothing but the truth so help him God, and stepped solidly up to the stand, affecting the air of a man torn from the important work of his day.

Glossing over the incident with his 'employee' and Joe Flick's mother, Cashman spun a tale of Joe riding up to the pub, armed and raving, taking delib-erate aim and 'missing' due only to the Grace of the Almighty. No one there doubted that Cashman was an eloquent and capable witness.

'I think Joe Flick was inspired by stories of bush-rangers and derring-do in currency with my clien-tele at the hotel,' said Jim Cashman. 'I think he is easily led, and subject to the whims of his emotions.'

When Joe was asked to present his side of the story his mouth clamped up, and he could not speak, cowed into silence by confusion, fear, and this terrible turn his life had taken. Various members of the court, including Hasenkamp, the clerk, and then the Magistrate himself attempted to cajole and gentle Joe into speaking, but he remained silent, shoulders hunched, and shaking visibly.

'Struck dumb by guilt,' called a heckler from the audience.

In blessed relief, they let Joe sit again, while Police Magistrate Lawson scribbled notes and re-read statements. Finally, he looked up, 'Will the prisoner now stand.'

Joe came to his feet, shaking in every muscle and limb, cowed by this first experience of English justice. He saw no pity on Alick Lawson's face, just self-belief in his role in delivering the law, a cog in the wheels of justice that stretched all the way to Queen Victoria herself.

'Joe Flick,' Lawson said. 'I have examined the evidence, and find that there is sufficient cause to believe that you did, most feloniously, attempt to murder Mister Patrick James Cashman. I commit you for trial on the twenty-second day of March 1888, at the Supreme Court, Normanton. Bail is refused.'

There was a smattering of applause from the audience, and a muted but heartfelt wail of anguish from one woman, right at the back of the room. It was Kitty herself, for she had, with Henry beside her, come to see her son face court.

From his place near the front, Harry Hasenkamp smiled, pleased that justice would be done, and a new commendation added to his service record.

And while the rain pattered down on the canvas tarpaulin I'd roped to four trees at Kitty's camp, to improve her living conditions somewhat, and so we could talk without getting wet, I marvelled at how fast lives can change. At how one thoughtless act can send a soul hurtling down the wrong path.

'We went along there that day in the Burketown courthouse, you know,' Kitty told me. 'Me an' Henry up the back. By an' by they bring Joey along outside. He couldn't look at my eyes, poor boy. What a thing for a woman to see the babe she suckled, there in chains, and all because he fought for her, because he loved his Mama and fought for her.'

'It broke your heart?' I asked.

'Yeah, my heart broke,' Kitty agreed. Her eyes became as weathered and old as the country beneath us. I saw something inside – a relic of the cycles of life, of mother and child, all down through the generations.

Kitty took up her pipe, and would not speak another word to me that day.

CHAPTER 5

Escape

HASENKAMP AND HIS MEN shackled Joe with iron chains, and escorted him 130 miles to Normanton, a four-day ordeal on horseback. Morning, noon and night they fed him on lumps of flour dough, seasoned with black pepper and boiled in water – a concoction known as 'hell-in-a-billy.'

By the time they approached the town's neatly surveyed streets, laid out on the western bank of the Norman River, Joe had calluses on his neck and wrists, and his spirits were so low that he could scarcely stomach food or water.

This was Kurtijar country; the people of the river plains. Joe saw them – men, women and children –

watching from the camps on the fringes of town as he rode in with his neck chain firmly and humiliatingly in place. The Kurtijar knew those police neck-chains well, and must have wondered what Joe had done to deserve his.

The Normanton lock-up was located behind the Police Quarters in Borck Street – a more substantial facility than Burketown's. It had an exercise yard, and four cells in a line. The judicial complex was built up on stumps, all solidly made of heavy timber slabs secured with iron spikes. The windows were too small for a goanna to shimmy through, and the iron door would have resisted a bull. The prison compound, in its entirety, was enclosed by walls lined with galvanised iron sheet, ten feet high.

Joe shared his cell with two other men. One was on remand for assaulting his wife. The other, a young Irishman, was serving thirty days for riding a horse without permission, and swearing at a policeman.

'They've charged ye fer the 'tempted murder of a white man?' the horse 'borrower' asked.

Joe nodded miserably.

'T'ey'll give ye ten t' fifteen year fer that. No question.'

'Ten to fifteen years in here?' asked Joe, gesturing at the bare cell.

'Not here,' piped up the wife-beater. 'They'll take you to a proper gaol. Townsville, probably.'

Those four walls crushed in on Joe, and his world reeled. The thought of being taken away, far from here, to a stone prison, seemed to him much worse than death. A despondent sense of doom settled heavily on him, and he huddled into a corner like a spiny anteater, digging into the earth, leaving just sharp quills exposed. Nothing could dislodge him; nothing could hurt him.

Joe stayed like that until late in the afternoon, when he had a visitor – the owner from Lawn Hill Station, Frank Hann, a family friend if there was such a thing for the Flicks. The station owner approached the cell, dressed in his 'flash' travelling gear – cream-coloured moleskins and a striped Crimean shirt. A nearby guard unlocked the door and let Joe out to speak with him.

'Hell, Joey,' Hann cried. 'What's this I hear about you shooting at Mister Cashman?'

Joe clammed up again. He didn't mean to; it just happened. He looked down at the ground and avoided Hann's eyes.

'I can't assist in any way, shape or form if you don't talk to me, lad.'

Still, Joe said nothing, arms folded protectively around his body, and eyes glazing over like window shutters. He wanted to go back inside the cell and be like an anteater again.

Hann went on, 'I hear your old man went and had a word to Cashman. Told him that there was no harm done, and that he should drop the complaint. Jim Cashman said he wouldn't, and well, I guess that's his decision.'

There was not even a flicker in Joe's eyes at the station owner's words.

Hann shook his head. 'I'll help if I can, but I don't think there's much I can do.'

Finally Joe found his voice. 'Fifteen years in a stone prison, for the little what I done? I can't face that, Mister Hann.'

'You just might have to, Joey, but wait and see, for the judge might sympathise, and I'll put in a character reference for you.'

The guard pushed Joe back inside with the others, and slammed the door. Heavy cast-iron doors, it seemed to Joe, sang a note deeper and more final than any other sound on earth.

In the late afternoon of the next day, when the sun was at its hottest, and the iron wall like a branding iron to the touch, the prisoners were allowed outside to exercise, under the eyes of two warders armed with Martini-Henry carbines.

Joe kept himself apart from the other inmates, now including a bunch of Burns Philp seamen who had been arrested the night before for drunkenness. He walked in aimless circles, shoulders slumped and hands in his pockets. So deep was his reverie that he did not heed it at first, a very distant, but high and piercing bird call from outside the prison grounds. When it came again, however, he stopped walking and listened – a clear twin whistle, with the second note higher in pitch than the first.

Every muscle and nerve in Joe's body came alive. That was the call of a quail-thrush, a creature of the mulga a thousand miles to the south. Joe knew that there was only one person who could so perfectly mimic that bird. Somewhere, outside those walls, was his mother, and she was calling him.

Joe looked at the guards. They had noticed nothing. Now he eyed off the walls. They were ten feet high, but someone had piled firewood for the kitchens quite close. If the stack held it could be used to help jump the full height of the wall, and Joe was not lacking in agility. The iron would be hot, yes, but his hands were callused from hard work.

He waited until the guards were distracted, one tamping his pipe, carbine held in the crook of his arm. The other man was trying to get a vesta to strike.

Sprinting towards the wall, Joe instinctively chose the right moment, jumped for the wood pile, then used his left foot on the peak to take a flying leap. He was a born athlete, and his fingers just managed to grip the top of the burning hot iron.

With a tremendous heave of his shoulder and arm muscles he lifted himself, his face contacting the hot metal in the process, yet his knee rising just high enough to find the top of the wall. Adroitly Joe's left foot came up, and for an instant he stood poised with both feet on the edge.

A rifle discharged, and a bullet stung through the air like a wasp. Joe cocked his knees and jumped, and for a young man who'd been thrown by rough horses since the age of five or six, landing safely on the hard ground was no challenge, using the flex in his legs and ankles to absorb the impact.

Wasting no time in recovery, he ran with all his considerable speed, heading into the sun, across the series of horse paddocks and outbuildings that made up the police reserve. Ahead he could see the start of the scrub. If only he could make it before the police were out and mounted up.

Joe's luck held. Within a minute he was dodging saplings and termite hills. His hearing was as sharp as a wallaby's, and again he heard the quail-thrush call. He altered his direction a fraction.

The bird call sound moved seemingly as fast as he did. It was eerie, almost supernatural. He reached a shallow gully, where the wattle and box trees grew more thickly, and was sprinting up the other side when the call came again from his left. He saw a fallen bloodwood trunk, and then his mother's face appeared from behind it, beckoning him to her.

He saw what she had done, hollowed a space in the soil beneath the decaying base – a small cave, and after Joe slithered in beside her, she raked a cache of branches and leaves into the opening.

For a long time there was silence. Twenty minutes or more. Then the sound of hoofbeats and shouting voices, close at first, then fanning out into the distance.

'They'll be back,' Kitty whispered.

'... and track me here,' Joe whispered, but Kitty shook her head and showed him the pair of his old boots that she had worn, crisscrossing the area, heading out in a dozen false trails. 'All night I done that,' she said.

Kitty was right, though, the police came back to search the area again. Mother and son lay close together, listening to the sounds of the hunt around them, often fading into the distance, sometimes very close. Once Joe saw a pair of police boots so near that he felt he could have reached out and touched them. Soon, however, the man passed on by.

After sunset, when the night was fully dark, Kitty and Joe left their hiding place.

'Listen good, Joe,' she said. 'You walk to Magoura Station. Missus Franny Trimble expecting you, and will be ready with horses and tucker. By and by you ride for Nicholson country, past Corinda. Your father is heading there directly, with plenty tucker for you to get to the Territory.'

'Where will I meet him?'

'You savvy that place close by Nudjabarra, the little waterhole, where we all three camp that time?'

'I know it.'

'That's where you meet Henry. Then he tell you where to go.'

Joe hugged her with happiness. He should have known that his family would look out for him.

Kitty again donned Joe's old boots. 'I'll lead 'em away,' she said, 'give 'em a good trail to foller up tomorrow.'

They embraced one last time, then Joe watched his mother melt into the shadows and disappear.
He gave her a start, then prepared for his departure. Travelling the eighteen miles to Magoura on foot, however, didn't appeal. Instead he worked his way from the scrub near the prison into the township, keeping to the shadows when he could, and avoiding the pubs.

With a race meeting scheduled for the following week, many of the contenders were already in town, being put through their paces on the track each day. Joe made his way out to the paddock in which several of these racehorses were grazing. He recognised the stallion Marathon, belonging to a carrier called

Darcy, a horse that beat the field every year at the Normanton and Burketown carnivals. He was a lively, spirited animal, just the kind that Joe loved to ride.

His next step, however, was to hurry back to the police station. Where else would he find the best saddlery in the township? The stable door was held by iron staples, but Joe levered them out as quietly as he could. Once inside he visited the tack room, selecting a saddle blanket, bridle and saddle. As an afterthought he chose a felt hat from a peg, and placed it on his head. Looking just like any bushman heading home, he walked openly down the street.

Marathon, in Joe's mind at least, seemed to be waiting for him to return, snuffling at the air expectantly. Hadn't Henry Flick said that his boy was part horse? Joe spent a minute or two stroking the stallion's neck, asking for and offering trust. The animal seemed to come alive at a sense of adventure in the offing, a change from the tedium of the racetrack. He stamped and snorted as Joe fed the bit into his mouth, tightened the chin strap, then gently positioned the saddle and buckled the girth.

Their friendship sealed, Joe walked Marathon with a loose hand on his bridle, through the gate and ever so quietly out of town, wrinkling his nose at the smells of civilised life, the smoke from kitchen stoves, cooked food, and chicken coops.

With a sense of leaving that settled world behind, rejecting it utterly, Joe swung up into the saddle, and set off for Magoura Station at a canter.

· CHAPTER 6 ·

Magoura

BEING INTERESTED IN THE original people of the Gulf and their culture, I often stopped to talk to Old Jack after my meetings with Kitty. He was a wiry fellow, knotted like old rope, with a sharp mind and an encyclopaedic knowledge of that strip of coast. Somehow, after a few of these conversations, I earned myself an invitation to take a ride in his dug-out canoe.

He told me to come early in the morning, when he predicted gentle breezes and clear skies. This forecast proved to be perfectly accurate, and he was already impatient to launch when I wandered up after my breakfast.

The canoe was some fourteen feet long, still with the marks of stone adzes along the interior. It was no lightweight I discovered when I helped Jack heave it into the water. Two carved paddles lay inside the hull, along with a dugong spear – a weapon some eight feet long, with a head barbed on one side, fixed to the shaft by tightly wound bindings.

Jack reckoned that we had little chance of spotting a dugong or turtle, for the water along the coast was coloured with wet-season outflows from the many creeks and rivers. Even Doomadgee Creek, as we called the western branch of Arthur's Creek where we launched the canoe, was flowing deep chocolate brown.

Stepping gingerly aboard, while Jack held the stern, I soon found that the craft was not particularly stable. After wobbling alarmingly at first, I learned to keep my weight to the centreline. Jack gave us a shove out into the stream, then clambered aboard with such agility that the canoe seemed as solid as the HMAS Canberra.

My guide took his place in the stern, grabbed a paddle, and I did the same, with the old man instructing me when to change sides. It was a fine feeling to fly down the channel, with the help of a strong ebb tide, while armoured crocodile heads surfaced amongst the mangroves, small baitfish skittered from the water, and kites or eagles took to the wing from tree-top vantage points on our approach.

Soon it was not a matter of paddling for thrust, only steering the vessel through the bends, and keeping it straight in the eddies and whirlpools. Soon we were racing out from between the mangrove-lined heads of the creek into the wide-open ocean, the hull thumping against a small chop.

I felt like an adventurer indeed, with islands scattered on the horizon, and the wide Gulf shore seemingly untouched by governments, empire builders and settlement.

After some half a mile of paddling in a westerly direction, Jack put down his paddle, took up his spear, and asked to exchange places. This we managed, somehow, without ending up in the water.

The next hour or more will remain like a cinema reel in my memory: Jack poised in the bow with his spear at the ready, peering down into the water and the sea surface around us, while I paddled gently onwards in the direction of his pointed commands. His dark skin was free of any trace of fat, every muscle in his shoulders and back portrayed in stark relief, broken only by scars left by his life as a hunter.

Once or twice I saw him tense, as if he had noticed some sign that was invisible to my eyes, but then he relaxed again. Eventually he sat down, chuckled and shrugged.

'Today, they live, and we go hungry,' he said, then indicated that we should exchange places again.

Later, when I arrived at Kitty's camp, she seemed a little put out that I had made a new friend from amongst her neighbours. She called Jack a few names that I dare not translate here.

Then, pausing only for the ritual of filling and lighting her pipe, she took up the story where she had left it the day before.

Sub-Inspector Patrick Brannelly, Kitty told me, was the officer in charge at Normanton at the time Joe made his escape over the wall. Brannelly had cut his teeth in the Royal Irish Constabulary before emigrating to Australia.

Brannelly had a close-trimmed beard, turning grey at forty-five years of age, a down-turned mouth that was inclined to sourness, and a hot temper. His intolerance for foolishness and time-wasting was legendary, as was his thick Galway dialect.

The evening of Joe's escape Brannelly was enjoying a drink with Brodie, Normanton's mayor, at Hely's pub. The barmaid had just mixed him a Bushmills and water, and he had scarcely lifted the glass to his lips when Sergeant Ferguson hurried in, touched his superior's shoulder and whispered into his ear.

'Excuse me sir, we've had an escape.'

Brannelly placed the glass on the table, then stood abruptly. 'Good Gahd man. An escape?'

'That's right sir.'

The room went quiet. Even Missus Hely herself, dressed in heliotrope silk, stopped her earnest study of her customers and the cash in the drawer and listened.

'Now tell me. Whech o' de despicable and low examples o' 'umankend behend ooehr walls ded manage to escape?'

'Joe Flick, sir.'

"Ow in de name o' Gahd ded 'e do it?'

'He jumped the wall, sir.'

"E joehmped a ten-foot irahn wall? Dat's a tall tale to be sure, sergeant. 'Ow lahng ago ded dis ooehtrage ahcur?'

'Ah, several hours sir.'

'And why was I naht tahld earlier?'

'We were trying to locate him sir, and we did not think it would take long.'

Brannelly downed his glass in one long swallow, then tapped his chest. 'I regret to say Mester Brahdie, dat me subardinates 'ave let me down.' He glanced sharply at the sergeant. 'Let oehs all down. Oenfahrtunately, I moehst leave you.'

The Inspector and his subordinate walked out the door, past a group of men showing off a giant mangrove crab trapped from the Norman River. The left pincer was clamped onto a stick, while the other opened and closed menacingly.

Ignoring the show, the policemen walked briskly back to the police station. The quarters were all but deserted, with most of the constables out looking for Joe.

Brannelly gathered the remainder, including any trackers left in their barracks, and gave them a tongue-lashing. 'You let a weld boehsh lad outwit you?' he cried. 'Get ahn yooehr horsches and fend

Joe Fleck tahnight. Fend 'im ahr be damned to ye all and start lookin fahr new jahbs.'

Not all the absent police constables were following false trails laid by Kitty. Others were smart enough to expect that Joe might equip himself with a horse and ride from town after dark. Some three miles out, something – a scarcely detectable scent or sound – warned Joe that there was trouble ahead. He slowed Marathon to a walk, then reined in and dismounted.

Moving onwards, scarcely breathing, he heard voices up the track. Leaving the horse tethered to a tree, he moved closer and saw the glow from a pipe bowl as someone inhaled. The smell of tobacco smoke struck his nostrils. Up closer he made out the buttons on a serge jacket, and the black line of a rifle barrel. Joe shivered with relief. If he had ridden straight on into the checkpoint they would have opened fire on him.

Doubling back, Joe rode up into the scrub, and bypassed the area, though he slowed his pace and moved more cautiously.

By dawn he had reached Magoura Station, crossing open downs studded with knee-high termite mounds, and a bountiful covering of Landsborough, Mitchell, and blue grasses. The cattle were so settled that they scarcely looked at horse and rider as they passed.

Magoura was one of the Gulf's finest cattle stations, a mix of freehold and leasehold, with ten thousand cattle feeding on the plains. Some eight hundred square miles in extent, it was watered by the Flinders River, and the Bynoe, a tributary.

The owner, one of the most respected pioneers of the district, Irishman George Trimble, had died after a brief illness the previous year, and his widow Frances was keeping the place going with a manager, an old and faithful head stockman called Holmes.

Joe arrived at the homestead in the mid-morning, snooping in slowly, in case the police were there waiting for him. There was no sign of them yet, however, and he rode up to the homestead. Holmes and the other men were out on the run, and as Kitty had promised, Frances Trimble was waiting for him.

She was tall and slight, with no figure to speak of. It was her habit to wear cattlemen's gear instead of a dress, doing any job the men could do, from dressing a bullock to breaking a colt. Joe had always liked her a great deal, and the sight of her kind face made him feel more hopeful.

'You're a young fool, Joey,' she admonished. 'Shooting at Mister Cashman was a mad act, even though what happened to your mama was despicable.'

'I know it was. I'm sorry, but I can't take it back.'

'No you can't, more's the pity. And where did you get that stallion, isn't he Mister Darcy's racehorse?'

'Yes, that's him. Marathon.'

'Yes. Well unsaddle him and let him go. Like as not he'll head home and you can choose a couple of mounts from here to take with you. Run in a mob from the horse paddock and have your pick while I bring out a pack and some tucker.'

The cook, a thin man with knobbly knees and greying hair pulled tight in a bun at the back of his head, was watching nonchalantly from the verandah, there rarely being such high entertainment as the arrival of an escaped prisoner on the premises.

Franny Trimble turned to him and cried, 'Hey you, Ah Fong.'

'Yes Missus.'

'Climb up on the roof and watch for horsemen on the track. If you see anyone coming call out. You understand?'

'I unnerstand, Missus.'

The gangly cook headed for the side of the house where he scrambled up a trellis, to the water-tank, then onto the roof, carefully keeping to the main beams and avoiding the unsupported grass thatch in between. Once he reached the ridge he made his way along to the chimney. There he stood, making a pantomime out of staring into the distance with one hand held parallel above his eyes to shade them.

'Keeping proper look out, Missus,' he called down.

Franny Trimble ignored him and went to fetch the tucker and pack she had promised.

Meanwhile with the help of a stockwhip that had been left coiled on a yard post, Joe ran a dozen station horses into the yards and made his selection, looking for good overall conformation, straight shoulders, depth in the chest and a spirit to match his own. Quiet horses were not Joe's thing.

Choosing two, he tacked up the best prospect, an active bay, and when Frances reached the yards they worked together to fit packs on the second, balancing them by eye as best they could.

'Nothin' yet, Missus,' came a shout from the cook on the rooftop, as if to remind them that he was still up there, doing as he had been bidden. Meanwhile Joe fitted Marathon up with a lead rope so he could string him behind the others.

'Aren't you going to let him go?' Frances asked.

'Yes, but not here. In case he hangs around and gets you in trouble.' Joe paused expectantly, 'Can you let me have a rifle?'

Frances considered the question then shook her head. 'No, Joey. I know you might have need of a weapon on the track, but if the police come up on you you're better off without one. Just give yourself up if they catch you. Promise me that.'

Joe was ready to mount up when a tremendous screech came from the cook on the rooftop. 'Missus, Missus. Mounted men coming this way directly. Four maybe five all-up.'

'How far away?' she called back.

'One mile, maybe more.'

'That'll be the police,' she said to Joe. 'I'll delay them for as long as I can.' She grinned. 'No copper alive can resist tea and scones. Now go, and the best of luck to you.'

Joe had no spurs, but his boot heels were hard enough. Even in a hurry, however, he retained his natural caution. He chose his route carefully, letting his horses' hoof-prints mingle with the countless marks that had been made when he ran in the mob. This done, he set off across the horse paddock, letting himself through a bush gate on the other side.

Keeping on a westerly heading, Joe stayed off the main trails, anti-tracking where he could. Even with the traps breathing down his neck, it was a good feeling to be on a fine horse, with another carrying enough tucker to get him to his father's camp at least.

It was only the lack of a weapon that bothered Joe now, and he turned his mind, as he rode, to how he might acquire one.

· CHAPTER 7 ·

Hunted

ONE MORNING AS I went about my work on the mission, I heard two of the children sitting in the shade playing a game, chanting in low voices. It was a dirge sung to the rhythm of a funeral march. I heard a name mentioned that froze my heart and I walked closer so as to hear it.

Joe Flick, Joe Flick, the p'lice shoot 'im dead;
Joe Flick, Joe Flick, he fell, he fell;
They bury 'im upside down; poor Joe.
Wild Joe gone to hell, to hell, to hell.

I had by then walked so close that the pair stopped their chant and looked up at me self-consciously.

'Where did you hear that?' I asked.

'In Burketown, Mister Morris. People sing it. Sometime kids.'

'Do you know who Joe Flick was?'

'No Mister Morris.'

'Are there any more words to the song?'

'No more. Are we in trouble Mister Morris?'

'No, not at all.' Yet, I made them wait while I fetched my notepad and wrote down those four terrible lines. I did not mention the verse to Kitty, though I imagined that she must have heard it, over the years.

Joe, as he ran for the rugged Border Ranges, learned what it was like to be hunted. Of every rocky outcrop hiding an ambush. Every traveller an informer. Trackers poring over each impression of hoof and boot; reading the sign each time Joe dismounted to eat or brew tea.

Joe directed his horse along shallow stony creek beds, walking his plant backwards up the banks, at intervals of hundreds of yards, before continuing on his way. He laid false trails to the north and south of his true path. He left red herrings such as horsehairs in bushes, reversed around large trees and set off in erratic directions; even slipped from his saddle while his plant plodded on, running on foot in a wide circle before re-joining them. These tricks, however, were time consuming, and good trackers would find the correct trail eventually.

Twenty miles on from Magoura, back on the main road, Joe passed the sign-posted track heading into Inverleigh Station. This sprawling cattle run was owned by Will Fleming, in partnership with a woman called Jessie Kennedy. Joe had done cattle work there in the past, and he remembered the storehouse behind the homestead where weapons were kept.

Reining in on the cross roads he considered his position. He was used to carrying a revolver at least, and if he were armed the police would have to think twice about tackling him. Everyone knew that trackers baulked at closing with armed men.

The decision made, Joe nudged his new bay gelding off the road, heading down to the creek that wound back towards the homestead. It was an hour before he stopped just short of the itinerant camp, in view of the homestead and outbuildings from the rear. Then, leading all three of his horses back into the waterside scrub, he tethered them within reach of shade and water.

Banking on the stockmen having gone out to work, and the servants being busy inside, he approached the storehouse. It was simple enough, he found with his strength and thin frame, to force an iron shutter and squeeze through. The interior was dark, but Joe's eyes soon adjusted. From a wooden rack inside he chose a .577 calibre Snider carbine. This he lowered to the ground out through the window, along with a box of cartridges. Heart hammering with excitement, Joe squirmed through and outside. There he flipped the hinged block out of the receiver, sliding in a cartridge and replacing the block. This done, he slung the loaded carbine over his right shoulder for ease of travel.

Keeping under cover as much as possible, Joe reached the horses again without being seen. He rode off the way he had come, finally re-joining the main route to Floraville. It was there that Joe decided to set Marathon free.

With the knots untied and the rope removed, however, the stallion wasn't keen on leaving his new friends.

'Ah, you can't stay with us, boy,' Joe muttered. 'Though I'd love to keep you … I promised Missus Trimble I'd let you go.' With those words he delivered a firm slap to the animal's rump.

Just at that moment, Will Fleming came down the track from Normanton way, riding casually towards him. Joe was not frightened; Fleming was better known for his skills at the game of chess than gun play. Yet the shock of recognition came quickly to the station-owner's face.

'Hey, Joe Flick,' shouted Fleming. 'Is that you?'

'Yah,' cried Joe, digging his heels in hard. He took off at speed, the packhorse following, leaving Marathon behind.

Will Fleming stared after them, wondering what the hell was going on, though anxious to report that he had just seen the wanted man.

Not sparing the horses, Joe travelled fast to the Nicholson, bypassing Corinda Station, then the Turn-off Lagoon waterholes, wheeling around the area with its smells of woodsmoke and beer, and the sounds of men at work and play. He saw a gang unloading timber from a dray, bullocks lowing and someone shouting. Joe had the sense of being on the outside now. They had locked him out, taken away his ability to participate in society.

Turn-off Lagoon was so named because this was where the two main Territory stock routes began. The inland path, across the Border Ranges to Fish River Station and the Barkly Tableland was called Hedley's Track, and the more northerly alternative was the Coast Track to Westmoreland Station, then Borroloola and beyond, a journey known for its fever, humidity and mud. A third road also started here; the route to Bowthorn Station.

Joe spent several hours heading up the coast track, then cleverly doubled back and went the other way, crossing the Nicholson upstream of the settlement, at which point he followed the river to its wild headwaters.

Finally, after twenty straight hours in the saddle, he left the main course of the Nicholson, and turned up a scrubby, rocky little creek. There he saw a smudge of smoke, and Henry Flick sitting beside a cooking fire, walking to meet him with a worried smile on his face.

Joe dismounted and grinned widely. 'Pa?'

The vine-dresser's son clapped his son's back, tut-tutting at the weight he had lost and the haunted shadows around his eyes.

Henry had a good beef stew simmering in the tin dish that also served as a gold pan, and before long Joe was eating his fill. There with his father he felt free for the first time since he had felt the bite of iron chains on his skin. Henry Flick had always been such an authority in Joe's life that the Queensland police now seemed about as potent as March flies and their hot needle stings.

'Where did you get the rifle from?' Henry asked while Joe spooned stew into his mouth.

'Inverleigh.'

'You stole it?' Henry Flick cast a sharp glance at his son.

Joe met it with a steady eye. 'Yes, and some cartridges. Fleming saw me riding away, so the "pinks" know I've got it. Should help keep them off my back.'

'We'll talk about that later.'

Joe put down his tin plate and smiled, teeth white in the firelight. 'Are you gonna ride with me to the Territory?' He could not hide his good spirits. With his father beside him he felt safe.

'No, I'm not coming with you, Joey.'

Joe took a long swig of tea from his pintpot, and looked sideways at his father. 'That's a shame. I would have liked to ride with you – and it's all new country for me.'

'That's true, but it's the road you have to take, Joey. You've done what you done and there's no way back. I'm here to help you, but my life is at Lawn Hill.'

'I don't really want to go to the Territory without you and Mama. How am I supposed to fit in there?'

'You're as good a man with horses and cattle as I've ever known.'

'That's not what I mean. I'm not one of the old people, and not white either.' Joe pointed to the south. 'Mama's country is a thousand miles from here. Maybe that's where I should go. Maybe that's where I belong.'

Henry Flick shook his head. 'Put that out of your mind, son. Look at me. I was born in Germany, but I was just a crawling babe when we sailed for this country, and I can't remember it one bit. I've lost touch with my family down south too. I heard that my old man – your grandfather – died just two or three years ago. It was too far for me to go. This is our country now – yours and mine both.'

'I'd give anything just to be back at our camp,' Joe sniffed, 'settlin' down around the fire with Mama tellin' her stories.'

'Well you can't do anything except make the best of it now,' said Henry. 'Life is not easy for anyone. And there'll always be people, like ol' mate Jim Cashman, who try to bring you down. Who try to stop you from being the man you need to be.'

'I'm scared,' Joe said at length.

Henry Flick did something he had not done for many years, he moved next to his son and drew him close, feeling the trembling in that hard, thin frame. 'I know that. Now stay just one night here – you know they'll be tracking you as we speak, and they never ever give up. Tomorrow you can ride on to the Territory – all the way to Hodgson Downs – Minyerri the old people call it. My mate, Jimmy Crawford is the manager. Just tell him that you're my son and he'll give you a job. You can lay low there.' He paused then said, 'I'm proud of you, Joey, for standing up for your mother. Whatever happens, I'm proud of that.'

And then, with Joe half asleep in his arms, Henry Flick sang a lullaby in his rough and gravelly voice – one that he remembered his mother Rosina singing to him through his childhood.

Wie ist die welt so stille,
und in der dämmrung hülle.
So traulich und so hold!
Als eine stille kammer,
Wo ihr des tages jammer
verschlafen und vergessen sollt.

How the world stands still,
in twilight's veil.
So sweet and snug!
As a still room,
Where the day's distress
you will sleepily forget.

When Joe finally moved to the swag Henry had prepared for him, he slept soundly, with his father keeping watch. In the piccaninny dawn he was breakfasted, mounted and ready to ride, while the chatter of wrens, spinifex pigeons and honey-eaters reverberated between the faces of that rocky creek.

Henry reached up to clasp his son's hand. 'Put all this behind you, Joey. We're counting on you to re-build your life.'

'I'll do my best.'

'One last thing,' Henry said. 'See that rifle, I want you to throw it in the creek.'

Joe laid a protective hand on the wooden stock. 'I don't want to.'

'Take the damn thing and throw it in the creek. It'll cause only trouble.'

Joe made a face, but he unslung the carbine and with a heave of his arms speared it far out into the waterhole, where it made a splash and sank without trace.

Then, with a last clasp of his father's hand, and many a backwards glance, Joe rode off towards the Territory. He was soon to rue the lack of that rifle, for it may well have prevented a wound that would almost take his life.

· CHAPTER 8 ·

Wounded

KITTY TOLD ME HOW her son Joe rode to the west in the wild upper Nicholson country, through a river gorge intersected with knife blades of red stone, ancient cycads and calm, clear pools rich with turtle and fish. She told me about Wanggala – the age of creation – when the river was formed – this artery snaking through the land.

She told me of a line of ranges white men called the China Wall, and the sacred dreaming places of the old people along the route. She told me how the Waanyi still talk of the turbulent years – the Wild Time – when the cattle moved in, and the trouble began.

Then she told me of how proud Waanyi men almost took her son's life, for Joe was riding a horse, wearing a hat. To them he was all the same as a white man: any man in Western clothes and mounted on a horse was a target, and especially one who dared to ride alone and unarmed into the border country.

By late that next afternoon, Joe reckoned that he must have crossed into the Territory, and he breathed easier. Back then, Queensland and the Territory were separate colonies, the latter being part of South Australia. The police could not move freely across borders and Joe felt safer from them, for the time being.

Joe was riding through cave country, slow going between rocks hidden by tussock-grass and spinifex, when three Waanyi spearmen, wearing head-pieces adorned with feathers, rose from the broken ground to his right. Another group appeared, blocking the track. Knowing some words of their language, Joe shouted that he was a friend, and meant them no harm. His knife seemed small and ineffectual, but he drew it anyway.

The terrified packhorse reared up, slowing any chance Joe had of burning them off with speed.

Spears flew, driven by long woomeras at the speed of a diving cormorant. Each of these weapons was some nine feet long, and tipped with a barbed and razor-sharp worked head of stone.

Joe deliberately jinked his horse, but a spear drove into his foot, cleaving through the leather of his boot, driving deep into sinew and flesh, then tearing out from the sheer weight of the hanging spear. The point left a bloody gash, and the pain was deep and shrill.

Another missile struck Joe's pack horse in the chest, and it kneeled, mortally hit, bellowing blood from its open mouth. Blanking out the pain, Joe turned and cut the lead rope, and kicked his mount onwards. Blood from his foot smeared its flank.

Joe aimed his horse, thankful that its courage matched his own, directly towards the group that had gathered ahead of him, one spear missing his head by a whisker. The thundering hooves of his gelding were lethal weapons in themselves, and the Waanyi parted, giving Joe space to gallop through.

He kept that pace up until his horse's sides were flecked with foam. Ten miles, fifteen, he rode, until finally he slowed enough to look at the wound in his foot. It was still oozing blood, and he felt weak and light headed. He took off his boot and bound the wound with strips cut from the only spare shirt he still had.

For three more days Joe hung on, with no rifle to get meat, scarcely with the energy to stay in the saddle, guessing himself to be on the Northern boundaries of the vast Alexandria Station. He plucked bush food when he came across it – billy goat plum from the tree, biting the tangy abdomen of the green ant, or grubbing for water lily tubers and mussels in the very few waterholes he came across once he left the Nicholson.

Finally, he struck the waving grasses of the Barkly savannahs – flatter even than the 'Plains of Promise' near Burketown, and easy going for a horseman. It was also possible to see a great distance all around, making him feel safe from mounted men. From here, it seemed, his best hope was to head for Brunette Downs, managed, at that time, by the famous cattle duffer Harry Readford.

In a forlorn condition, Joe followed a faint smudge of smoke from a distant cooking fire. Near sundown, a week after his break-out from Normanton, he stumbled on a stock camp on Corella Creek. It was just a bark hut and set of bush yards, with a white man leaning in the doorway smoking a pipe. A couple of black girls in stockman's gear were hanging around a fire.

'You're Joe Flick, aren't you?' the white man cried, walking towards Joe. He was of medium height, with brown hair and eyes, wiry rather than solid, but with an athletic air about him. 'Everyone's heard about your escape, and they said you might ride this way.'

Joe could see no point trying to hide his identity. 'You guessed it. But I'm hurt. I got speared in the foot on the Nicholson.'

The stranger looked at Joe's foot, swollen and wrapped in cloth to keep the flies off. 'The cheeky wretches! I thought Jack Watson had dealt with that lot.'

'Please don't give me up,' Joe pleaded. 'I'll do anything but go back behind bars.'

'No chance. My name's Charlie Gaunt, by the way.'

The names of these white men seemed to cause Kitty pain. She hugged herself with her arms and looked down at the smouldering fire, the bones and skull of a catfish slowly turning to charcoal in the embers.

When I asked her who Jack Watson was, she screwed up her face and spat tobacco-stained spit into the dust. 'Bad man. By and by head stockman at Lawn Hill.'

I later researched something of Watson's life, finding that he was a private school boy from Melbourne with a reputation for cruelty, who nailed black ears to the walls of the Lawn Hill homestead, and cleared whole river valleys of the old people, as Kitty called them. His come-uppance came later, when he was taken by a crocodile at Knott's Crossing, Katherine.

'What about this Charlie Gaunt?' I asked.

Kitty shivered, despite the heat of the day. 'Another bad one. Charlie Gaunt a killer too. But he help my Joey.'

After a pause to collect her thoughts, Kitty continued with the story.

'We heard you were on the run,' said Charlie Gaunt, 'and you'll get only assistance from me and Ned here – I've no love for that tight-fisted mongrel Jim Cashman, and don't get me started on Hasenkamp.' Another white man appeared from inside the hut, smelling of rum, bleary eyed and tousled.

'Here's Ned,' said Charlie. 'Heat some stew up for Joe, will you mate? He's done in.'

Joe tried to dismount, and would have fallen in the process, had the other men not come forward to catch him. They laid him out on Charlie's own swag, while Ned heated some tucker and the 'boys' saw to Joe's horse.

Unwrapping the wound was a trial, for Joe's hastily applied cloth had stuck to the wound like treacle. Each turn caused a shudder in Joe's body and a soft whimper of pain. Once it was finally uncovered, however, Ned took the bandages outside and burned them, while Charlie asked Joe to wiggle his toes, making sure that the tendons weren't damaged. When this was done he used hot water to bathe the wound, soaking away the pus and half-formed scabs.

'How bad is it?' asked Joe.

'Bad enough, but I've seen worse,' said Charlie, folding a belt and passing it to Joe to chew on, while he swabbed whisky onto the wound. 'We'll do the same again tomorrow. You're young, and you'll heal.'

For eight days Joe stayed in the camp, with the very few visitors from outlying cattle camps sworn to secrecy about his presence. At first, however, he could scarcely sleep with nervousness.

'Don't worry about it,' said Charlie. 'No man around here believes you should have been charged for what you did, and now you've told me what happened I think it even less.'

Joe was soon well enough to sit around the fire in the evenings, listening to Charlie Gaunt tell his stories of great cattle drives; of fights and massacres. Ned's tucker was good, and there was no hint of a threat, yet there was something about Charlie Gaunt that made Joe nervous.

Each day he forced himself to walk with a stick to hurry the healing of his wound, and he was impatient to ride, though he knew that turning up at Hodgson Downs half-crippled would make the manager think twice about hiring him.

Finally, however, when he could walk well enough, and ride even better, Joe decided that he was ready to continue his journey. The thought of working again as a stockman, living a normal life, appealed to him, and he knew that his father's mate at Hodgson Downs would do right by him. Henry

Flick had few friends, but the ones he had were like brothers.

Before Joe left, Charlie gave him a rifle, cartridges, three good horses, and a pack full of tucker. 'Hodgson Downs is two hundred miles from here,' said Charlie, 'and if Crawford is expecting you so much the better. No one will ever hear a word from us.'

Joe shook hands with both men, then rode off into the grasslands, countless seed-heads turning to gold with the morning sun.

· CHAPTER 9 ·

Hodgson Downs

AGAIN THE MONSOON RETREATED, and apart from storms bustling out from the horizon in the evening, the weather was better. I had my first touch of Gulf fever, but Dorothy Akehurst's store of quinine kept it at bay, and I remained on my feet most of the time.

I fished for barramundi in the creek, using a cat-gut line, and small fish for bait. Hussein caught these for me using a cast net that he had made himself from plaited pandanus strands. Once or twice I caught huge saw sharks, with proboscises studded with razor-sharp teeth, and while most people in the itinerant camp were happy to eat them, they had some significance to old Jack as a creation-being, and he would clamber down the bank, help me to cut the hook free, talking to the strange and primeval creature while we gentled it back into the water.

Barramundi, trevally, and catfish were all welcomed by the Akehursts for the mission kitchen, and I'll always remember how the children would skip along beside me while I carried a silver-scaled barramundi up from the creek, gill rakers cutting into my fingers, while Stanley and Willie whetted their knives to prepare this welcome change from beef.

Kitty was proud of my efforts, and boasted to the others that she'd somehow trained up my fishing skills. In any case, she beamed at me when I brought her down a chunk of fillet, though she liked turtle better, she told me.

After settling the fish-flesh on the coals to cook, she started to tell me how, a few days after leaving Corella Creek, Joe watered his horses in the stunning calm of the wide blue Anthony's Lagoon, jewel of the Barkly Tableland. After satisfying himself that there were no police in attendance, he dared to walk up the grassy hill and into the cluster of sly-grog shops and bark shanties that made up the settlement.

This was true frontier country, where men wore revolvers in their belts. Card games went on in the shade of casuarina and ghost-gum trees. Fights broke out on the street. Horses were swapped for women, and land deals were done on the backs of envelopes.

The store Joe approached was scarcely worthy of the name, but the shelves had not long before been replenished by dray from Newcastle Waters. Joe limped a little as he headed inside.

After selecting a sack each of flour and tea, then a smaller one of salt he fronted the counter.

'On account, please mister,' said Joe, bold as brass.

The store keeper planted his elbows on the counter and narrowed his eyes. 'And whose account would that be?'

'Sub-Inspector Brannelly, of Normanton,' said Joe without hesitation. 'Some constables an' the rest of us trackers are camped down Kilgour River way, trailing one true bad feller from Queensland.' He lifted one finger to his lips. 'But shhh … big secret.'

The storekeeper hesitated only for a moment, then shook Joe's hand. 'Tell your boss that the rations are on the house, and that I hope you and the constables get your man, whoever he is.' He lowered his voice to a whisper. 'And if that man happens to be the fugitive Joe Flick that goes double.'

Joe gave a knowing grin, lifted his finger to his lips once more, and backed out of the entrance.

Kitty, forty-odd years later, threw back her head and laughed, holding her belly to stop it jiggling. Then she continued with the story.

Joe, Kitty told me, fell in love with the Minyerri country long before he reached the homestead itself. The western reaches were broken limestone ground, rugged and beautiful, and the river itself a ribbon of silken green, sweet for cattle and men alike. Mitchell, Flinders, kangaroo and blue grasses grew on the better soils of the plains, and horses thrived.

James Crawford, the manager of Hodgson Downs Station was a fierce Scotsman in his late forties. 'I'm helping yew, Joe, for the sake of yer father. He's a guid man an' a true mate. Me own help depends on 'ow yew be'ave from now on. Yew try a trick like pointin' guns at people an' that help comes to an end. I'll give yew twenty shillin's a week an' all found. We'll call you Peter, and no one need ken where yew came from.'

Within a week, 'Peter' had proved himself to be an exceptional horseman and one of the cleverest cattlemen Crawford had ever seen. Joe was set on proving himself, and showed no interest in the usual stockmen's diversions of drinking rum and kidnapping Alawa girls.

Before long he was a trusted hand, both in the cattle camps and the yards. Back at the homestead, he took whatever corner of the men's camp was given him, and he ate whatever tucker the cook cared to dish up. Travelling with cattle was no hardship for Joe, and he never missed a night watch, shirked or complained. If there was a rush he was the first man onto a night horse and the first man to 'bend' the herd.

Arriving just in time for the station muster, Joe joined in the preparatory work of running in horses, shoeing, repairing or plaiting new hobbles, ropes and bridles. Saddles were oiled, and tucker packed for the camps.

Mustering on Hodgson Downs was carried out in sections. It was too big an area to muster in one go. The strategy, in the main, centred on the waterholes, where mobs of cattle would drink daily.

After establishing a camp, and knocking up some rough yards, the men would mount up at dawn, fanning out for miles around a huge area of pasture. This done, they would bring the 'net' back in, cracking stockwhips and shouting, herding wild cattle that might not have seen a horseman since the previous year's muster, if at all, along their usual pads or trails to the waterhole. Intractable, evil-tempered 'piker' bulls were thrown and tied, or if all else failed, shot.

On the banks of the waterhole, usually by noon, a dinner camp was made, while a couple of horsemen quieted the mob. Soon afterwards, the drafting and branding started. And in the mayhem, with hooves thundering, dust and smoke rising to the sky, and stockwhips cracking, someone would shout as a game weaner broke from the mob and a mounted man galloped close after, guiding the animal expertly back to the fold. This was no place for weaklings, and black men and white worked together as physical equals.

Joe, soon heading up his own team, had a favourite waterhole to work from. It was very long, narrow and brown, and curved in a gentle archer's bow to the west. Later, when Joe had gone from the station, and his true identity known, this waterhole was named by those who wished to remember him as Flick's Hole.

Weeks passed in hard but thrilling toil, and one night a travelling Queenslander turned up at Joe's camp and asked to speak to him privately. They stood on a knoll just near the camp with the sun glowing red in a smoke-tinged dry season sunset.

'Relax,' said the man. 'I know who you are but I won't give you away. I've got a message from your mama. She says that she sends big love to you, that she and your old man are well. What answer shall I take back to her?'

'Say that I love her too.'

'That's all?'

'Nah, also tell her that I wish I was home but that things are good here. Tell her I'm alright.'

The Queenslander had other news too. One of Joe's horse-thieving mates, William Haynes, had just been sent up for ten years on a charge of shooting with intent, and Monaghan Wilson had left the area.

The man rode away in the dawn, and Joe's heart felt warm from his mother's soul brushing his across the distance, with the magic of a few words. He went back to his work with a will. The Queensland police seemed to be a long way behind him.

As the season lengthened, the plains were practically exhausted of new cattle to muster. The stockmen moved their camps into the limestone country, where the rocks, hidden by dry kangaroo grass, were sharp as needles, and escarpments rose on every side.

The cattle here were feral, and with fewer waterholes to work from, coacher herds of quiet stock were used as focal points for the muster. Many of the free-ranging beasts had to be shouldered to the ground by horse and rider. Some small mobs, that had seen horsemen come and go before, sought refuge in the least accessible crags, and the men who brought them in with spur, rein and stockwhip were true artists of the range.

Once the newly-mustered cattle were in with the coachers the mob was usually over-excited and rampaging mad. At that stage the horsemen would circle around them, over and over, talking or singing quietly, watching for any attempts to rush or escape from the mob.

Not everyone in the camp appreciated Joe's skills. One man who became jealous of the admiration others felt for the young Queenslander was called Clarence Jones, a heavily built South Australian. He spent most of his days doing as little as circumstances permitted, interspersed with occasional acts of great daring and bravado that cemented his reputation and quietened grumbles about his lazy ways. Cruel with horses, women, and dogs alike, he was not popular in the camp.

The thing a shirker hates most is a natural. The man who does everything well, and is humble besides, never drawing attention to himself, but is respected through his sheer reliability and talent. Joe Flick, then known as Peter, was such a man.

One night, towards the end of the season, Joe's crew were in camp, eating johnny cakes and fresh beef, while the night watchman controlled the herd. The head stockman had just ridden up, and paid Joe a compliment about the excellence of the day's muster.

Clarence Jones stewed for a while, then started musing aloud. 'It's strange, you know. How we hear that a yella boy called Joe escapes from the Normanton lock up, then a month later Peter rides into Hodgson Downs. A hell of a coincidence, don't youse all reckon?'

Joe said nothing, and neither did any of the others. Those who had come to see him as a mate merely lowered their eyes in sadness. Most had worked that same coincidence out for themselves some time earlier. No more was said that night, or the next.

In the Wet season, while most of the ringers rode off to Darwin or Katherine, Joe stayed on, living the life of an honest stockman. The most intense work of the year was done, but there was plenty to do: breaking horses, plaiting greenhide ropes and yard-building. There were even a couple of late season grass fires that Joe helped fight, shoulder to shoulder with Crawford and his family, while dry storms crackled in dark clouds overhead.

Clarence Jones, meanwhile, happened to ride through Roper Bar on a roundabout way to the Katherine for an end-of-year spree. He called in at the store, then happened to catch sight of a poster showing a sketch of Joe Flick, and the words WANTED on the noticeboard out the front of the police station.

'Oh, that's "Peter" over at Hodgson Downs alright,' said Jones to himself, cradling the jug of rum he had purchased to assist him on the long ride to more civilised parts. He took the poster down, walked inside the police station and addressed the constable lounging behind the counter.

'I know where this yella dog is hiding out,' said Jones, holding up the poster.

Mounted Constable Stott sat up – yet another Scotsman, this time from Kincardineshire. 'Yew can tell me where Joe Flick is?'

'Sure can.'

Stott smiled, 'Well laddy. If yew're not jest blatherin' yew'd best sit down an' tell me where.'

• CHAPTER 10 •

Under Arrest

MOUNTED CONSTABLE ROBERT STOTT of Roper Bar, Kitty told me, was something of an enigma – maligned by some, and lionised by others. On his police record were awards for courage, yet he was once fined for brutally striking a Chinese boy who had disobeyed an instruction.

Born in a blacksmith's loft in Nigg, Kincardineshire, Stott was an ambitious and capable lawman. He had joined the South Australian police not long after his arrival in Australia, and soon requested a transfer to the Territory, chasing dreams of adventure and exotic landscapes.

Even though he now knew the whereabouts of Joe Flick, and was keen to add this arrest to his growing reputation, Bob Stott was nothing if not patient. The rivers were flooded, so, knowing that the fugitive would not stray far, Stott bided his time. He was a man who did things by the book, and a warrant was required.

Finally, when the Wet Season floods had begun to recede, Stott took a leisurely ride up along the Roper track to the Elsey. From there he telegraphed Palmerston, seeking a warrant for the arrest of Joe Flick on charges of escaping lawful custody in Queensland. The request was duly facilitated by the Commissioner, Paul Foelsche.

A week or two later, a mounted constable rode south, bringing the warrant, but also prepared to stay and assist in the capture of Joe Flick. Red Lily Lagoon was the agreed rendezvous, and there Bob Stott made camp with his trackers. The man with the warrant rode in the next day, and the two comrades hailed each other, catching up on the news while their trackers hobbled out the plant and pitched tents.

The newcomer, Friedrich Wilhelm Haedge, anglicised to Frederick William, was, like Hasenkamp back in Queensland, a second-generation German.

He was a solid horseman and a tough customer. Stott was glad to have him on hand for the arrest of Flick.

Red Lily Lagoon was a beautiful sight – a vast sheet of still water – fringed with reed beds, and dotted with lily pads and their flowers. Thousands of waterbirds floated or fossicked on narrow legs in the shallows. Pig-nosed turtles touched their snouts to the surface, and on the banks, agile wallabies flirted with the visitors, torn between curiosity and caution.

Haedge shot a goose, plucked it and arranged it on a wooden spit to roast over the coals. Then, he pulled a round bottle of Franken wine from his saddle bags and Stott matched it with one of whisky. Before long Stott was slapping his new mate on the back and calling him a gentleman.

'Have you a plan of how we'll bring this rascal in?' Haedge asked.

'There's one a' him an' four of us, wit' the trackers,' said Stott, 'so it shouldna be tae hard, but I've devised a ruse that should put him at ease.'

The next day the two policemen and their trackers rode downstream along the Roper track for the first few miles, then turned off towards Minyerri. All had revolvers and rifles loaded, in holsters and scabbards.

The afternoon was well advanced when they reached the homestead. Not attempting to hide their approach, the policemen rode in on the main track, right up to the verandah, where James Crawford waited for them with a pipe in his mouth.

'What brings yew lads this way?' Crawford called.

'Serious matters indeed,' said Stott, dismounting and greeting his countryman with a handshake. 'T'ere's been an attack on Newcastle Waters homestead by a mob a' Jingili spearmen. We're formin' a troop tae ride over an' put an end tae the mischief.'

Of course this was a ruse, but it was enough to get Joe off guard. Unsure of whether the officers were coming for him or not, he had been hiding behind an outbuilding. When he heard that they were not after him, but were looking for men to ride with them, he came out in the open.

'Hoy there Jack,' cried Crawford. 'Are yew keen on a mission of righteousness?'

Joe slowly walked towards the verandah, hands in his pockets. He wasn't keen at all. In fact he had no desire to go anywhere at all, most particularly not as a member of a police attack party.

'So 'tis man is Peter,' said Stott. Then, peering down at Joe, 'I've heard that yew're a braw stockman. Come up here an' throw down a drink, then we'd be pleased if yew'd ride with us.'

Stott himself walked to the waterbag hanging from a verandah post, and filled a tin pannikin for Joe, who had slowly made his way up the steps and was standing, still hesitantly, next to Crawford.

When Joe accepted the pannikin and took a sip, Bob Stott seized him from behind, while Haedge whipped out his revolver, and levelled it at Joe's face.

'You're under arrest for the escape of lawful custody in Queensland, Joe Flick,' Haedge bellowed. 'Come quietly or we'll bury you here, and save everyone a pile of trouble.'

'Yew sneakin' belters,' said Crawford, red in the face and furious. 'Yew'll take t'e ablest ringer in the Territory from me, an' fer no gid reason?'

Stott scowled and twisted Joe's arm viciously behind his back. 'T'is lad here is Joe Flick … a criminal, a lag on tae run. Are yew saying you'd already ken his identity? T'is a criminal offence tae harbour a fugitive from t'e law.'

'All I ken is that this man here, called Peter. Is a good an' honest lad an' is no more a criminal than yew an' me. Now ease up on him, yew're hurting him.'

Stott relaxed his grip on Joe's arm a tad, but addressed Crawford. 'Dinna stand in ta way of justice, James.'

'Whose justice, English justice? You should be 'shamed a' yersel', you're a disgrace tae yer countrymen, arrestin' honest men fer to make yer own self look big.'

Bob Stott was starting to lose his temper. 'I'll ask ye again. Did yew ken that this 'ere Peter was Joe Flick? If so we'll arrest ye too.'

'Nah,' muttered Crawford, backing down. 'I didna ken.'

'Weel shut yer trap an' leave it there.'

Joe, for his part, felt like a wallaby caught between two bushfires. He wished with all his heart that he had leapt on the back of the nearest horse as soon as he had seen the police coming. His self-protective instincts had dulled over his time here.

Stott read the warrant that Haedge had brought down from Darwin. Every official word hammered down on Joe, until he seemed to be surrounded by a thick fog. He said only, 'I am your prisoner, am I?'

The two policemen burst out laughing, deciding then and there that he was soft in the head.

Haedge led him off the verandah and out to where the trackers were readying travelling chains. Joe did not, at that time, think to wonder why they charged him only with escaping custody, rather than the original charge of attempted murder.

That strange omission was to have terrible consequences for him later, but Joe had no idea of that now. His first and only thought was how he might get away from these men at the first opportunity.

· CHAPTER 11 ·

Escape at Mount McMinn

BOUND BY LIGHT CHAINS and an iron collar, Joe rode just behind the two policemen, deep in a state of bitter recrimination and disbelief. The horse he'd been given was flat from work, and Stott constantly wheeled back to slap it encouragingly on the rump with a switch.

'There'll be nae hanging back an' trying to run fer it,' warned the policeman, lifting a calabash pipe from his lips with one hand, and gripping the reins with the other. 'I ken ever' trick in ta book, even tae ones that 'aven't been invented yet.'

That first day they followed the Hodgson River up to the junction, often at a distance to avoid rugged riverside hills, finally reaching Roper Bar after dark. Joe spent the night in the police lock-up there alone, pacing the cell from back to front, looking for a weak point he could exploit to escape.

Meanwhile, Stott and Haedge celebrated the arrest with whisky and loud singing from the police quarters just a stone's throw away. By morning Joe's fingernails were bloody from trying to prise sheets of tin away from the cypress frame, and his eyes had sunk deep in their sockets.

Joe's hosts slept late, and from dawn onwards, local ne'er-do-wells, brumby runners, unemployed ringers and seamen from a barque at anchor in the river came to look through the peephole at the caged fugitive. They made comments about the colour of his skin, and the circumstances of his escape from Normanton, while Joe hissed at them from the shadows at the back of the cell.

Around ten-thirty the policemen rose, chased the sight-seers away and packed for a long ride to Palmerston. Joe was fed and exercised outside. He again submitted to the chains, though he was given a change of horse.

'Mount up an' let's ride,' shouted Stott. 'We're Palmerston bound, to deliver a true rascal onto the scales of justice.'

Joe's chains stayed on all through the afternoon, as they followed the river track westwards. On the Roper's south bank, near the towering bluff faces of Mount McMinn, the party stopped for the night, in a campsite that had been used by drovers and other travellers for at least a decade, and for perhaps fifty thousand years before that by the Mangarayi people of the Middle Roper lands.

It was a picturesque bend of the river – a safe crossing place – with the channel narrowing around a bar and sand spit on the other side. A couple of 'gators scurried for the water as the mounted party approached. Still with his chains on, Joe was given a shovel and made to dig a latrine for the white men behind some screening bushes.

'Deeper,' cried Haedge, covering Joe with his revolver. 'Put your back into it. No man wants to look at another's turds while he squats.'

'It'd be easier without these chains on,' said Joe.

'It'd be easier without wastin' your breath complainin',' retorted Haedge.

Joe grunted with effort, and finally finished the hole, passing the spade back to his guard, who shepherded Joe back to camp. Stott was nearby, still busy with the trackers, hobbling the plant and relieving the packhorses of their loads.

'You need a hand there?' asked Haedge.

'Nae lad,' said Stott. 'We're all but done.'

Joe saw that Haedge had half turned his back on him. To encourage this carelessness he sat down on a stump near the fire with his head in his hands, looking like he was too fatigued from digging to pose a threat.

After a sharp look back, Haedge moved closer to Stott. 'I'll set the prisoner to cooking some tucker then. Might as well make him useful – he looks ready to drop from just a bit a' spade work.'

If Haedge had not chosen that moment to repeat a dirty joke that had been doing the rounds up in Palmerston, Joe might not have tried anything. The joke, however, ended with both policemen laughing, eyes closed and doubled over.

Taking this opportunity, Joe leapt to his feet and sprinted away, chains jangling as he went. He headed south, away from the river, back along the little detour that they had taken from the main track, then towards the towering, forbidding cliffs of Mount McMinn itself.

Shouts came first, 'Halt, or I'll shoot.'

The report of a revolver followed, the slug from which Joe heard collide with a tree trunk some ten paces to his left. The solid boom of a rifle discharge followed soon after, but by then Joe had covered some ground, reaching thicker scrub, changing direction, hearing the whinny of a horse back at the camp as a rider prepared to mount.

Joe ran like he had never run before, ignoring the weight of the chains and the drag they made on his muscles, mingling blood with sweat where the collar cut deep. Prison to him seemed worse than death. He could not bear the thought of going back. Not after he had spent so long proving himself at Hodgson River.

The sun was glowing deep red as it dipped into the river valley to the west, and Stott had no choice but to take one tracker to chase Joe, leaving the other with Haedge to protect the plant. More than a few escapees on foot had been known to double back and cut out a police horse.

'Thank God there's a guid moon,' said Stott, 'while I fetch this wild lad back.'

'Take care out there,' said Haedge.

'I'll be back in an hour, wit' Joe Flick on 'is blasted knees.'

And Stott rode into the south with the tracker, a strapping Yuruwinga man called Paddy from the border country around Lake Nash, a fierce and competent figure in his own right.

Paddy was a clever tracker and afraid of nothing. He was also mounted, and took the lead, leaning down from his saddle so his eyes were close to the ground. After a half mile he sat up and turned back to Stott. 'Joe Flick movin' plenty fast boss.'

'Then we move faster. Tae weight o' ta chains will tell on him. We'll run tae cheeky belter down.'

Over the following hours, the light gradually lessened, until the tracker sometimes lost the spoor and had to cast around to find it again. Joe was anti-tracking as best he could in the circumstances, using wagon-sized boulders of bare stone as thoroughfares to hide his tracks as they neared Mount McMinn itself.

'It's like he jump-off into the air,' said Paddy.

But the speed of the horses told against a man weighed down with iron.

Stott's saddle clock was showing close to nine pm, when Paddy hissed that he could hear Joe's chains close by. The constable slipped from his horse and followed on foot. Now and then they heard a jingle, but echoes from the stone were deceptive.

A stone flew from nowhere with the speed of bullet, striking the policeman in the small of the back. Stott cried out with pain, then whirled in all directions with his Colt aimed at the night. 'Where are ye? Are yew a damned ghost.'

The policeman walked onwards, the tracker just a dozen yards ahead. Joe's right arm had a deadly aim, and uncommon strength. Another swish of air and a stone flew close past the policeman's ear.

'I'll tan yer hide, lad,' warned Stott, but another stone struck him a glancing blow high in the forearm, almost forcing him to drop the revolver. They were deeper into the broken country beneath the cliffs now, and Stott began to despair, for if the terrain grew any tougher they would be forced to leave the horses.

Paddy, however, walked back and handed the reins of his horse to Stott, then leaned down to whisper in his ear. 'Joe Flick up there on the rocks. Me-feller go up an' flush him out. Wait, then by 'n' by go on – all the same ready.'

While Paddy climbed up a rough staircase of sandstone, expertly picking his way around a wild tangle of turkey bush and stone, Stott tethered both horses to a nearby branch, then walked slowly on. Every sense was alive, waiting for the stone that might fly from the darkness and strike him down.

Then, emerging from between two slabs of rock, Stott found himself on the edge of a clearing. A moment later there came the thump of a jumping man landing, the clang of chains, then Joe running across that moonlit space.

'Stop, in the Queen's name,' called Stott.

When Joe failed to stop Stott fired twice above his head. This not being effective he took careful aim at Joe's back. At extreme pistol range, and in bad light, his bullet was guided only by luck. There was the thump of a slug striking flesh; a cry, and the sight of Joe crumpling to the ground.

'Got him,' exulted Stott. He hurried forward with the gun raised. Joe lay in a patch of bloody grass, writhing like a clubbed goanna, wounded in the back. Stott kicked him in the side of the head.

'Lay still, you young cur.'

Paddy came up beside the policeman, and the two men, white and black, stood over Joe's injured form. Both were thinking the same thoughts. That it would be so easy to put one more bullet in Joe. Dig a shallow grave and save everyone a great deal of trouble.

Stott, however, believed in justice. He believed in the system. When Joe's struggles subsided, the constable knelt, took a cursory look at the wound, and plugged it with a handful of dirt. 'It doesn't look mortal,' he commented. 'We'll fetch him back to camp.'

The two men laid Joe's shaking, bleeding body over Paddy's horse, and thus carried him five miles back to camp. Joe was shivering with shock, pale in the firelight as they propped him against a tree, with a blanket draped all the way up to his chin.

'He looks near jiggered,' Haedge commented.

'Not yet. But he's lost a pint or two of blood.'

Joe's eyes opened and he saw his captors around the firelight, felt the chains that still bound him, and at that moment he wished with all his heart that Stott's bullet had taken his life.

· CHAPTER 12 ·

Fannie Bay

TELLING THE STORY OF Joe's wounding distressed Kitty. The sandy blight that afflicted her eyes – that near blindness – made her somewhat inscrutable. Yet as I grew to know her better I could tell when the howling dog of grief inside her slipped the leash and brought her down.

Kitty explained to me that she did not blame Joe for running. He had grown up as free as any boy alive, at home in the woodlands and savannahs, the red gorges, the clear waters and dark paperbark swamps. Then, after being chained and dragged away like an animal, the policeman's bullet tore through his flesh, leaving him bleeding and weak.

To Kitty, her son was the hero of this tale. Hadn't all the trouble started when Joe stood up for her against a predatory man? Hadn't he done only what every son should do? Everything that happened from that moment was as much a part of Kitty's story, as his.

Joe's wound had only half healed when they set off again. Stott's bullet had struck at an angle, burrowed in through the meat of his back, hit a rib and torn back out, leaving a bloody wound but not harming the vital organs inside.

Within a week the police party were back on the track north to Palmerston, and the mounted constables took no chances with Joe from then on. At every stop he was chained to a tree, forced to sleep sitting up or half lying with the links stretched tight and the collar pulling at his neck. In Katherine he languished in the lock-up for three days, his wound still leaking blood and fluids while Stott and Haedge rested up and drank beer and whisky at Barney Murphy's pub.

In the middle of April the party arrived in Palmerston, and Joe had his first experience of a real prison. Fannie Bay Gaol was built from porcellanite stone, quarried from Doctor's Gully, and was imposingly solid, shut off with iron and rock from any view of the bay or Point Emery. Most of the inmates were black, others Chinese and a few whites. Many were on trial for their lives. The hangman was busy in 1889.

Two warders greeted Joe and his escort for a formal handover. His details were recorded. He was showered, his hair cut, and prison clothes issued. As was the custom he was placed in a cell alone for observation before joining the general prison population.

When they opened the barred door of the 'welcome' cell for him, Joe hesitated. This was the natural reaction of a man who instinctively knew a trap when he saw it. The warder saw this hesitation as insolence, and pushed Joe so hard between the shoulder blades that he flew inside, sprawling against the far wall, crushing his lip, tearing the wound in his back afresh.

The door slammed shut behind him. The warders laughed and wandered off, leaving Joe lying on the floor. Sobbing with pain he finally lifted himself so he could sit on the cot. The humid air was foetid in his nostrils. New prison sounds reached his ears: someone screaming; a voice raised in anger; a distant stationary steam engine huffing and cycling. Occasionally the smack of a whip or baton, or the sound of a distant snare drum as soldiers marched at the garrison.

After perhaps an hour, a new face appeared at the door. It was a white man in late middle age, with drinker's veins on his cheeks and bulbous nose. 'You're the Queenslander, aren't you, Joe Flick?'

There was something kind about the man, so Joe looked up and nodded.

'The guards here are mostly mongrels,' said the warder. 'But you've got nothing to fear from me. My woman and me, we have a lad. He looks a lot like you. Me name's Tommy Cook.'

Almost a whisper: 'Mine's Joe.'

The man's face creased in concern. 'That's blood on your shirt.'

'Yes.'

'I'll get you in to see Doctor Wood at the infirmary. Leave it to me.'

'Thank you.'

The doctor treated Joe kindly, tut-tutting over the wound, binding it tightly with clean bandages, and berating Haedge and Stott, in their absence, for forcing him to travel before the flesh had healed properly.

'Now watch out Joe,' warned Doctor Wood. 'They'll put you in a cell with three others tomorrow. The gaol is so overcrowded that they're squeezing four men into cells designed for three. Wash your hands every time you use the privy, and be careful what you drink and eat. Dysentery and typhoid fever can kill you, and both are rife here, do you understand?'

'Yes sir.'

The next morning Joe was taken to a cell with three other men, one of whom had been convicted of robbery with violence on the Pine Creek goldfields; another was a deserter from the British Navy, and the third a Welshman who would say nothing about who he was or what he had done. The latter spat on the floor when Joe arrived. They did not want the extra man, no matter who or what he was. There was no floor room left. No space to walk. The cell was twelve feet long by twelve feet wide, with exactly twelve feet of ceiling space – a perfect cube. The latrine bucket was in one corner, in view of all.

The day started with the clang of a bell at seven am. At this stage all prisoners had to make their beds, then stand for inspection as the warders walked through. Then, when the cells were unlocked, the prisoners shuffled through to the dining hall for a breakfast of oatmeal porridge. In the mornings most of the prisoners were expected to work, and Joe was assigned to the prison garden, chipping out weeds with a hoe under the watchful eyes of men with rifles. At noon there was bread and tea. Then two hours in the exercise yard. Those two hours kept Joe alive. He walked the grass in bare feet, with the green stalks soft between his toes. He talked to no one, and instinctively avoided forming any association. He shunned confrontation, turning away when the gaol toughs tried to rile him up.

On Thursday, April the 18th 1889, Joe was cuffed and escorted to the courthouse, in the company of a Northern Territory policeman called Corporal Waters. When Joe's case came up he was brought into the dock before Justice TK Pater who glared down at him with kindly, but authoritarian eyes.

Justice Pater was from a distinguished English family. His grandfather had served under the Duke of Wellington, and Pater had himself been a London barrister before emigrating to Australia. Known for a quirky nature, and for saying much more than his masters would have liked, Pater wore a full black beard and 'flash' clothes.

Corporal Waters stood and was sworn in. He said: 'I produce a telegram received from the Commissioner of Police in Adelaide, which states the offence and gives a description of the prisoner, Joe Flick. I also tender a copy of the Queensland Police Gazette stating the offence committed.'

Mounted Constable Bob Stott was next to take the stand, and his story was simple. 'I am a mounted constable stationed at the Roper River. I arrested the prisoner on a provisional warrant at Hodgson Downs on the 28th day of March.'

'Very well,' said Justice Pater, his voice a slow and gravelly drawl. 'Do we have a representative of the Queensland police here to take charge of the prisoner?'

'Not yet, your honour,' said Waters.

'Have they been informed that he is here?'

'Yes, sir, they have.'

Justice Pater's eyes hardened with some indignation. 'Well it's not up to us to feed and clothe every Queensland fugitive that comes our way. Tell them that they need to hurry up.' He banged his gavel down, 'Joe Flick you are remanded in custody for seven days pending representations from your state of origin.'

Joe was taken back to his cell, still in some pain from his wounds, full of fear at what would happen. He lay on his bed, staring at the ceiling. Seven days. Just seven days then back to Queensland. He didn't want that, but how could it be worse than this place?

Two days after the court appearance, Joe suffered the first chronic stomach pains. Within an hour he was on the bucket, face contorted, and the emissions would not stop. By midnight they had no choice but to take him to the infirmary, half walking, half carried like an invalid.

There Joe lay, for three days, curled up like a baby, shaking with pain from his gut, while every bed filled, emptied only when those who had died from the full-blown typhoid fever that ravaged the gaol were carried away.

Tommy Cook looked in on Joe every day, reading to him from slim books he carried in his pocket: sometimes poetry, and occasional adventure stories from exotic places. Tommy was with Joe when he returned from the hospital to his cell. Only three men slept in there now, for the Welshman had died of typhoid during the week.

The court process ground away. British justice was as unstoppable as time. Corporal Waters came for Joe again the next Thursday, and he was again handcuffed for the walk to the courthouse.

Justice Pater glared down from the bench. 'Has a representative of the Queensland police arrived to take Joe Flick?'

'Not yet, your honour.'

'Have they expressed any intention of doing so?'

'No sir, but we have written to them again,' said Corporal Waters.

Pater made. 'The prisoner is remanded for a further seven days, but let it be known that I am not impressed.'

More diarrhoea, more days of cramping pain followed. On the following Saturday the prisoners, fifty-three in all, were marched to the exercise yard to watch a fellow inmate who had struck a guard three times around the face and head, being whipped.

The charge was read aloud by the head warder. The miscreant's shirt was removed and he was tied to the whipping post. A guard took a cat o' nine tails from a calico bag, and whipped the man until his back was in bloody shreds.

The following Thursday came, and still no officer from Queensland had arrived.

'Do they intend to come for the prisoner at all?' asked Justice Pater.

'I have received a letter saying that they will despatch an officer of the law to collect Joe Flick as soon as arrangements can be made,' said Corporal Waters.

Pater shook his head, 'I am heartily sickened by this business.' He looked down on Joe. 'It is not fair for any man, no matter what his crime, to be hauled up every week and kept in suspense as to his fate. Especially since Joe Flick has not yet been convicted of any crime! Still, at this stage I have no choice but to continue this farce.' A bang of the gavel. 'Remanded for a further seven days.'

Weeks passed, all of May and June. In prison Joe's wound slowly healed, but dysentery revisited him time and time again, though he avoided the more serious typhoid. He was bashed once, by two men who didn't like the way he 'slunk around' the yard.

His cell mates came and went. He was called a yella mongrel and a half breed.

Each Thursday Joe was hauled up before Justice Pater. Each time it was established that no one had yet come to collect the prisoner. Each week he was remanded in custody for a further seven days.

Finally, by the end of June, the long wait became too much for Justice Pater. 'I must again express my extreme dissatisfaction with the behaviour of the Queensland Police.' He looked down at Joe. 'If they do not send someone to collect you by the time you appear before me in seven days' time, I intend to set you at liberty.'

Joe had scarcely spoken a word in that courtroom. Now, however, he looked up at the judge, his eyes liquid with hope. 'You'll set me free?'

'If they do not come for you, I will.'

Three days later, Tommy Cook walked towards Joe in the exercise yard. His face was grave. 'Joe, I've got bad news. Constable Harry Hasenkamp just arrived on the steamer to take you back to Queensland.'

Joe sat down on the grass, face in his hands. The new hope that had filled him drained away, leaving only bitter despair.

· CHAPTER 13 ·

A Dirty Trick

RAIN!

Not since the Great Flood could such a deluge have fallen. We endured days when it barely let up at all. The rise on which the mission stood again became a real island as the salt-pans filled, joining with Arthur's Creek. The grass turned a vivid green, and the sky a battle-smoke grey.

Conditions, overall, were unpleasant. Our clothes remained ever damp and reeked of mildew. Day and night, the frogs and bugs never ceased their cacophony. Pythons and other snakes competed with us for space and caused constant fright. A salt-water crocodile took Len Akehurst's best laying hen from just behind the mission house. One of the older mission girls ran after the reptile, prepared to belabour it with a garden stake, until reliable Lizzie restrained her.

Kitty and I continued our meetings under the sheet of canvas with which I had equipped her camp. Thus protected from the rain she told me how, when her Joey was in the Territory, she rode from the mining camp all the way into Burketown where she walked into the Watson Brothers' store and asked Robert MacGregor 'Greggy' Watson to read her anything relating to Joe in the newspaper.

Even when he was busy, the kindly shop-keeper would pour Kitty a cup of tea and sit her down on the bench seat that ran along the store front, deep in the shade of the verandah. Court news from Darwin dragged on for so long that it became quite the talk of the town, and most people thought that Joe should be released.

'They won't let him go,' warned Greggy Watson. 'They never do. Joe doesn't even have a lawyer to speak on his behalf.'

'How we get Joey one of them?' Kitty asked.

'Money,' Watson explained, rubbing his thumb and forefinger together.

Kitty rode back home, and together she and Henry figured how much cash they could get their hands on. A cheque had just come from Frank Hann, including some back pay, and Henry had two small gold nuggets, won in a game of poker in Central Queensland, that he had been carrying in his swag for ten years.

Still not knowing if it was enough to pay a solicitor, they rode together to Normanton. Henry first arranged to sell the nuggets, then left Kitty on the street with the horses while he walked into Heley's pub. There he addressed the bar, pleading his son's case and collected another three pounds ten shillings from well-wishers. The total sum he converted to a teller's cheque at the Queensland National Bank.

Their final call was on the skipper of a ketch, anchored in the Norman River and intending to sail with the morning tide for Port Darwin. The man was known to Henry, and they trusted each other.

Henry pressed the cheque into the skipper's hands. 'I need you to take this to Palmerston for me. I want you to find the best lawyer in that town and give him this. It's for our boy Joey, so he can be saved.'

On the twenty-ninth day of June, 1889, Constable Harry Hasenkamp swaggered down the gangplank of the SS *Catterthun* onto the Government Jetty near Fort Hill. He cast an appreciative eye on the town up on the ridge, and with his kit bag on his back, navigated the Chinaman's Walk up to Cavenagh Street.

The township of Palmerston seemed like the height of civilization to Harry. Even the chaos of Chinatown seemed like a nice change for the bush policeman, and the town seemed calm after Normanton, where recent events had stretched his nerves, and the police presence to the limit. This was part of the reason the response to Joe Flick's arrest had been so slow.

It had all started on the fourteenth of June, during a festival being celebrated by Normanton's South-east Asian population, near the town wharf. A Javanese man named Sedan used the noise made by the revellers as cover to creep up on a tent in which two European travellers, Christian Menager and John Fitzgerald, were reading by lantern light. Their forms were no doubt silhouetted through the canvas.

Sedan, a cook and waiter from Rafferty's Hotel, had armed himself with two twelve-inch daggers. Without warning, he stabbed one man through the tent material. His mate ran to the tent flap to see what was happening and copped a knife to the chest for his trouble. The Javanese then mutilated both victims with multiple slashes, only desisting when a third man, Davis, came to investigate.

The killer set upon the newcomer, wounding him in a dozen places, severing fingers, opening wounds in his legs, piercing his heart, ripping open his bowels and almost severing his head.

It was not Hasenkamp himself, but his comrade Constable O'Keefe, who made the arrest the next morning. Sedan did not seem concerned at the bite of the handcuffs on his wrists. 'Oh, you hang me – you shoot me – I don't care,' he said.

A brisk hanging would have been the end of the matter except that the local white population, outnumbered by Malays, Javanese and Filipinos, saw the attack as a conspiracy and were afraid that they might be the next to die.

Deputations to the Police Magistrate requesting that all people of Asian extraction be arrested had no effect. A public meeting followed, in which the police agreed to swear in special constables. The white petitioners, unimpressed with the result, went on a rampage, burning all 'alien' houses to the ground.

The irony that many of the rioters were themselves born overseas, albeit in the British Isles, must not have occurred to them. Sergeant Fergusson and his policemen felt themselves unable to do anything but stand and watch.

Finally, the Police Magistrate gave in, commandeering a barque at anchor in the river, the *Rapido,* and ordering the arrests of all South East Asians in the town. Sixty-four men, women and children were subsequently deported to Thursday Island, and from some reports they were starving by the time they reached it.

All in all, it had been a difficult few weeks, and Hasenkamp was pleased to leave town. Now, in Palmerston, he enjoyed something of a hero's welcome, for the Territory's German-born Commissioner of Police, Paul Foelsche, greeted the Queenslander as a countryman and colleague, providing digs at the police barracks, and dinner that night at his residence. They drank wine, ate bush turkey baked in the oven, and spoke of progress, justice, and civilisation.

The following day Hasenkamp made arrangements to collect Joe Flick as soon as his case could be squeezed in. The hearing was booked for the following Tuesday, and passage arranged on a steamer two days after that.

That same afternoon, the warder Tommy Cook opened the door of Joe's cell, and with him was a man in a suit and frock coat.

'Joe,' said Tommy. 'This is a solicitor. His name is Mr John Joseph Symes, and he's going to try and help you.'

Joe looked up at the lawyer. He was in his mid-thirties, tending to jowls, but with an intelligent spark to his eyes. 'Isn't it too late, now that Hasenkamp is here?'

'Perhaps,' Symes said honestly, his Dorsetshire accent still strong after more than a decade in Australia. 'But I've received some money from Burketown … your parents and some other sympathetic parties, I believe.'

That news alone – knowing he was not forgotten – was enough to lift Joe's spirits. He walked with Symes to the visiting room, where the solicitor began by telling Joe a little about himself. He had been admitted to the Inner Temple in London while still a young man, and had bought passage to Adelaide out of sheer curiosity and the need for a new challenge. After a few years in the southern capital, the same quality had brought him to Palmerston. 'It's not fair, what's been done to you Joe. I'm here to help.'

'Can you get them to set me free?'

'Probably not. But you can be sure that I will scrutinise Hasenkamp's every move, and if there is a legal challenge to be made, I will make it. Now, I want you to tell me every single thing that has happened since the day you committed the alleged offence …' He looked at Joe. 'Since the day you fired your revolver in the direction of Jim Cashman.'

Joe did not look at the man once as he told his story, only at a patch of blue sky through the bars of the window.

On Tuesday Joe appeared in court for the extradition hearing, and Justice Pater's eyes glistened with sympathy. After all, this was the prisoner he had so nearly released.

Joe tried not to look across the room at Harry Hasenkamp, but could not resist a glance or two. That strong jaw and arrogant glare dominated the court room.

'Constable Hasenkamp,' said Pater. 'Have you come for the prisoner, Joe Flick?'

'That I have.'

'Swear him in, Bailiff, and let's get this business over with.'

The bailiff brought out a King James Bible and swore Hasenkamp in. When it was done, the policeman gave the following statement: 'I am a constable in the Queensland Police Force, at present stationed at Normanton. I know the prisoner Joe Flick. I arrested him on the thirteenth day of March last year on a charge of attempting to murder James Cashman. The arrest was made about fifty miles from Burketown. He was brought before the court there, and committed for trial on the twenty-second of March, at the Supreme Court, Normanton. No bail was allowed.

'Joe Flick was escorted to Normanton gaol. I have tendered the depositions taken at the Police Court before Mr. A. Clarence Lawson, Police Magistrate. On the first day of April last year, the prisoner made his escape from gaol. I, and many others, were in pursuit of him for some time, and followed him towards the South Australian, (Northern Territory) border. I now intend to take the prisoner back to Normanton to stand trial.'

Pater called Joe's solicitor. 'Mr Symes, have you any objection to the handover of your client?'

'I do not sir, provided that the Queensland officer shows the court the warrant he is carrying for that purpose.'

Hasenkamp looked confused. 'I have already tendered a warrant.'

Symes chimed in. 'Yes, Constable, but that warrant is for Attempted Murder. Joe has not been charged with that crime in the state of South Australia, only Escaping Lawful Custody.'

Justice Pater wiped his face with his hands, then glared at Hasenkamp. 'Mr Symes is technically correct. Unless you produce a Queensland warrant for Escaping Lawful Custody I cannot hand the prisoner over.'

Hasenkamp paled. 'Your honour, I have no such warrant. I didn't know it was required to be for the specific charge.'

Pater folded his arms. 'Is that so? How long have you been in the police force?'

'I have been in the force for about seven years. I did not know that a provisional warrant had been issued for prisoner's arrest in the Territory. Furthermore, I have had no experience in such business before today and my commanding officer, Inspector Douglas, did not inform me of such requirements.'

'Well,' said Pater. 'Here are the facts. I will not let the prisoner go without the correct warrant, and in fact I was on the verge of releasing him. Get the warrant with all despatch, or I will make good my promise to him.'

Another four weeks passed. Another four court appearances, and each time John Joseph Symes ridiculed Hasenkamp, increasing the pressure on Justice Pater.

'The warrant is coming,' said Hasenkamp, time after time.

Still no new warrant arrived.

Finally, on the 27th of July, Justice Pater swept into the court with a new sense of purpose. 'Do you, Constable Hasenkamp, have the required documents?'

'No your honour. The judge is out of Normanton at the present time. We have sent to Brisbane, but it may still take another week.'

Joe looked at the policeman. There was something sly about the crooked grin on his face. It made him afraid of what might happen next.

Symes stood. 'Your honour. I wish to remind you that in the last four months my client has been remanded in custody sixteen times. Sixteen times he has been taken back to his cell to rot. You cannot let this travesty continue.'

'You are right, Mr Symes,' said Pater. He fixed his formidable attention on Joe, 'I'm very sorry for what you've been through. I am releasing you now. You are free to go.'

Joe looked up. 'I can just walk out of here?'

'That's correct. Corporal, remove the cuffs!'

Joe glanced again at Hasenkamp. The Queensland policeman still did not look disturbed. It was as if he still had something up his sleeve.

Once the cuffs had been removed, Joe thanked Symes, then walked down the aisle, pausing only to say good bye to Tommy Cook, who was in the gallery.

Fielding curious stares from bystanders and officials, Joe walked out of the courthouse and into the mild dry-season daylight. No one moved to stop him. Then, as he left the main door of the courthouse, he looked back to see both Corporal Waters and Constable Hasenkamp following him.

He had a terrible feeling of impending disaster. He did not feel free. The two policemen hurried to catch up with him. Joe felt a strong hand grip his arm.

'Not so fast,' growled Hasenkamp, twisting Joe's hand behind his back, and slapping on a handcuff.

'What are you doing? I've been released. The judge let me go.'

Corporal Waters took over. 'You were arrested for the charge of Escaping Lawful Custody, and for that you have been released. I'm now rearresting you in the state of South Australia on the original charge of Attempted Murder, for which Constable Hasenkamp holds a Queensland warrant. You are going back to Normanton, Joe.'

The sound of the rain on the sheet of canvas that covered that portion of Kitty's camp became a roar in my ears.

'Oh, the sodding mongrels,' I said. 'How could they be so dastardly?'

Kitty looked down at the ground, where a small channel of rainwater was snaking through near her sleeping place, carrying fragments of grass, leaves and the small, powerless, bodies of ants along with it.

· CHAPTER 14 ·

Of Steamers and Saw Blades

A LETTER FROM SYDNEY arrived on the *Noosa*, when she next chugged her way up Arthur's Creek to the Doomadgee landing. My supervisors had written to enquire of the progress of my thesis and to request the despatch of a substantial report. Time was slipping away, I realised, and over the following days I put in a serious effort to complete this task, despite my fervour to hear the rest of Joe's story from Kitty.

My handwritten dictionaries of the Waanyi and Gangalidda languages now exceeded three thousand words, though there were aspects of sentence construction and general grammar rules that eluded me. I practised my skills on Stanley and Willie, often provoking fits of laughter at my earnest but misguided attempts to speak as they did.

More time passed than I had anticipated, and the next time I went down to Kitty's camp, a couple of fresh plugs of tobacco in my pockets, it was deserted, the ashes in her fireplace cold. Jack admitted to taking her across the floodwaters to the other side in his canoe. I asked him where and why she had gone and he just shrugged and muttered something about 'she 'goin' walk to see if the bush plum all the same ripen up.'

Yet, there was more to it than that, I could see in his face.

For some weeks Kitty was absent from her place near the creek. I despaired, not only for her, but of ever hearing the rest of Joe's story. The only positive was that I continued to apply myself to my work, and I spent my spare time noting down the details of Joe's story that she had already told me.

Then, one day in early March, Kitty returned, walking across the still-boggy saltpans. I saw her coming, a lone stick-figure in a glare of white haze.

She was, I soon found, thinner even than before, but seemed to have regained some inner peace.

I gave her a day or two to recover, then took her a fresh-baked loaf of bread, some tea and tobacco. She was keen to talk, settling down by the fire, filling her pipe and asking me questions about happenings at the mission while she was gone.

Then, her pipe drawing nicely, she settled down on a ragged old tartan blanket and started to talk.

Harry Hasenkamp, she told me, along with Joe, boarded the SS *Catterthun*, a steamship bound for Southern Ports. Pride of the Eastern and Australian Steamship Company, the *Catterthun* was a two-thousand-ton iron passenger steamer, three hundred feet long, and with a crew of mainly Malays and Chinese. I heard that she later sank off Port Stephens, New South Wales, with a significant loss of life.

The brig was a steel enclosure, surrounded by pipes carrying water and steam, seething-hot all day and night. Joe, joined occasionally by drunks or disrespectful seamen, remained there for the duration of the voyage, chained on the orders of Captain J Miller.

Hasenkamp, meanwhile, enjoyed the facilities of the second-class lounge.

At Thursday Island Hasenkamp and his prisoner were transferred to a smaller steamer, the Black and Noble-built *Truganini*. At two hundred and three gross tons and with a beam of just twenty feet, she was one-tenth the size of the Catterthun.

The *Truganini* had no brig, and Joe was chained to a pipe near the funnel, vomiting into a bucket from rough conditions and the yawing, pitching progress of the steamship.

In Normanton, as they came off the boat and onto the main wharf, Joe saw that a crowd had formed outside the Burns Philp warehouse. Some had gathered to welcome loved ones but most were there to gawk at Joe, before heading back to their glasses of beer at Rafferty's Hotel.

As he passed, Joe saw Kitty and Henry, both waving, faces tragic. His heart beat like the hooves of a galloping horse to see them again.

The moment didn't last. A police wagon was on hand to carry Joe to the Normanton lock-up, and Joe managed his first wry smile in some weeks to see that the height of the wall had been raised by some three feet in preparation for his return.

Sub-Inspector Brannelly had recently been transferred to Croydon, and it was Inspector Douglas, formerly of Georgetown who took possession of the prisoner. All the local constables turned out to watch, while Joe was forced to stand on the front verandah of the police station, still chained and wearing Territory prison fatigues.

'Joe Flick, we are pleased to bring you back into custody from which you so feloniously did escape,' said Douglas,

Joe said nothing, just looked at the ground so fixedly that Douglas barked at Hasenkamp to grasp the prisoner's chin and drag his eyes up. This was done so roughly that Joe all but fell, earning himself a clip on the side of the head.

'That's better,' said Douglas. 'You've caused us all a deadly deal of mischief, but I hope you understand that running from the law is pointless. And that respecting the rule of law must become the cornerstone of your life.'

Joe had dropped his eyes again, and a great deal of trouble was taken by two men to not only raise Joe's eyes, but to forcibly waggle his chin up and down as if to say yes.

Douglas, tired of the intransigence of the prisoner, ordered him to be taken and incarcerated until a court date could be decided. Joe was unchained, marched out the back inside the enclosure, and placed in Cell Three. The door slammed closed behind him.

The sullenness left Joe. His mood was different. Seeing first the familiar bushlands on the banks of the Norman River, then Kitty and Henry, had awakened a fire inside his heart.

He prowled. He glared. He vowed that these walls would not contain him.

'You must be Joe Flick,' said a voice.

Joe turned to see a much older man with a long grey beard, an unlit clay pipe in one hand. 'And who are you?'

'I'm Ted Bell, you might have heard of me when I was on the road with a bullock team.'

Joe's eyes narrowed suspiciously. 'What are you in here for?'

'I lighted a shanty afire on the Saxby River – drunk as a king when I done it, an' the German shanty keeper was burned to death.'

Joe paled, his own crimes seemed minor in comparison. 'They've charged you with murder then?'

'Yeah, but that's not all,' admitted Bell. 'I'm charged with murder, arson and rape. I'll prob'ly hang from a rope before the month is out.'

Ted Bell gave Joe the creeps, and his desire to leave that cell grew stronger. He paced the floor, looking for a way out. The walls were solid, sheathed with sheet metal. The windows were lined with iron bars three-quarters of an inch thick. It was only the floor that gave him hope, for the cells were set up on stumps. The boards were two inches thick, but in one corner the termites had been busy, and the wood was not as strong as it had once been.

'If you're thinking of breaking out,' said Ted Bell. 'Count me in.'

Joe nodded, but he was already deep in thought.

The following day, Joe was remanded in custody by the police magistrate, and a court date set. Joe behaved well in the exercise yard, and caused no trouble. Within the week he was allowed visitors. Kitty and Henry hurried in on the very first day that this restriction was relaxed. There was no visiting room, just a few chairs in a corner of the yard, near the water tank.

Mother and son embraced until the gaoler tried to separate them, but Henry growled. 'Leave 'em alone. She hasn't held her boy for sixteen long months, and who would cleave a mother from her own flesh and blood?'

When their time was up Joe and Kitty embraced again. He whispered in her ear. 'Please help me. I need a thin, light saw blade. Throw it over the wall down the southern end, and I'll find it when they let us out at exercise time.'

This of course, was a dilemma for Kitty, for she had seen what happened last time she had incited Joe to escape. The sensible thing was to let him take his punishment. But there was something powerful at work now. Joe was on a course that she could not control. If she refused to supply the saw blade he would try some other way. She had seen in Joe's eyes that he had reached the end of his forbearance.

Strangely, when Kitty and Henry left the gaol that day, no sooner had they walked outside, to where their horses were waiting out the front, that Kitty fell to her knees, and let out a terrible wail.

She told me that it had suddenly struck her that she would never see her boy alive again.

The saw blade that Kitty threw over the wall the next day, was fine-toothed and flexible, made for a small coping saw and scarcely adequate for the task. The cutting of the boards, furthermore, was impossible to attempt without involving Ted Bell.

'I don't care if you escape with me or not,' said Joe to his cell mate. 'But keep your mouth shut.'

'I won't say a word,' said Ted Bell, 'an' like as not I'll follow you out.'

The sawing made noise, so Joe was forced to do his secret work only in the time between lockdown and lights out, when there was still activity in the cells. He also had to be careful not to break the tiny blade. Each night he disguised his work with saw dust mixed with soap.

On the third night he left just enough material to hold the planks in place, then lay in his cot, feigning sleep until the small hours of the morning. He slipped out of bed, pushed the two sections of floor timber through to the ground, then woke his cell mate.

'I'm going now. Follow if you want to.'

With nothing to take but the clothes he wore, Joe slithered through the hole in the floor, then wriggled under the building, emerging near the station's back verandah. Getting out of the enclosure was the next problem, but Joe had a plan. He hurried to the rear of the main barracks building, where on one side stood a galvanised iron water tank. He opened the tap, letting the water drain out onto the grass.

While he waited, he saw Ted Bell emerge from under the cell block, then lost sight of him in the shadows. He didn't care, the water tank idea was his, and he didn't want to share it.

When the tank was empty, Joe silently tipped it onto its side and began to roll it towards the wall, where he intended to use it as a ladder.

Ted Bell, in his work as a bullock driver, had made money by carefully weighing options; profit against risk; effort against return. Before blindly following Joe, he wondered if it might not be better to buy himself a bargaining chip for when his case came up in court.

Sounding the alarm that Joe was escaping was just such an opportunity. Surely the judge would look kindly on him for doing so, and he had no real desire to live the rest of his life on the run for murder. Without any further thought, keen to act before the moment had passed, Ted squeezed through the gap, wormed under the building, and slunk through the shadows, around the corner of the police quarters, finally rapping on a police constable's barred window.

Joe, desperately preparing for his escape, turned when he heard a commotion. The back door of the police station opened.

'There he is,' cried Ted Bell to the half-dressed troopers who accompanied him. 'I told you that he was escaping!'

Joe redoubled his efforts, pushing the tank against the wall, clambering up, using this extra height to grip the top of the extended wall. He tumbled up and over the Normanton gaol wall for the second time, landing safely, rolling and getting up. Unlike the last occasion he did not look for a hiding place or a horse, he just ran down the empty streets, heading for the scrub at the southern end of town, away from the river.

Before thirty minutes had passed he was two miles away, starting to anti-track as he went. Already he could hear the sound of hoof beats in the distance as mounted police galloped on his trail. Then, worse, the sound of dogs barking, taking his scent.

With sweat running down his face, and his breath coming in torrid gusts, Joe swore that he would die rather than be captured again. That he would never wear an iron chain again as long as he lived.

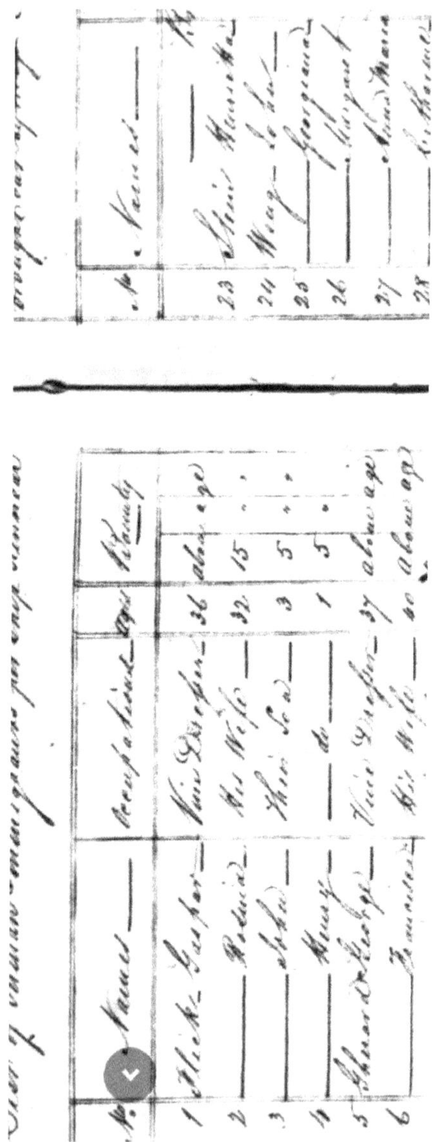

The Flick family's arrival in Australia.

Hut at Old Doomadgee (Vic Akehurst)

Frank Hann (SLQ)

Burketown in the early days (SLQ)

HenryHasenkamp
Photo taken during
his internment in
WW1. (Australian War
Memorial)

The Brook Hotel

1889. **DEATHS in the District of** Burke.

No.	DESCRIPTION. When and Where Died.	Name and Surname, Rank or Profession.	Sex and Age.	(1) Cause of Death. (2) Duration of last Illness. (3) Medical Attendant by whom certified, and (4) When he last saw Deceased.	Name and Surname of Fa[ther] and Mother (Maiden Surn[ame]) if known, with Rank or Profession.
1071.	23rd November 1889 Allsbridge Street Croydon.	Albert Edward Wood Primitive Methodist Minister	Male 23½ years	Enteric Fever (1) Intestinal Haemorrhage Exhaustion (2) 10 days (3) Dr. James (4) 23rd November 1889.	William Woo[d]
1072.	29 October 1889 Sawn Mill Station	Joseph Flick Stockman	Male 29 years	(1) Bullet Wounds Shot by the police in the execution of their duty. (2) (3) (4)	Henry Flick Miner
1073.	27th December 1889 Green Street Normanton	Mary Jackson Infant	Female 1 month and 2 days	(1) Spina Bifida (2) From birth (3) Dr. Dyson (4) 27th December 1889.	William Jacks[on] Carpenter Johanna [illegible]
1074	Supposed to be early part of the year 1883. North East of Dunbar Station Mitchell River.	Supposed to be Walter Clarke	Male about 30 years	Supposed to be (1) Murdered by Blacks (2) (3) (4)	
				(1) (2) (3) (4)	

in the Colony of QUEENSLAND, Registered by Clement Arnett Collard.

(1) Signature of District Registrar. (2) Date, and (3) Where Registered.	IF BURIAL REGISTERED. When and where Buried. Undertaker by whom certified.	Name and Religion of Minister, or Names of Witnesses of Burial.	Where Born, and how long in the Australian Colonies, stating which.	IF DECEASED WAS MARRIED. (1) Where, and at what (2) Age, and to (3) Whom.	Issue, in order of Birth, their Names and Ages.
(1) C. A. Collard (2) 20th December 1889 (3) Normanton	24th November 1889 Croydon Cemetery R. Montgomery	Revd Wm Howard Witnesses R.P. Hosken Robert Meehan	Yorkshire England 12 months in Queensland	(1) (2) (3)	
(1) C. A. Collard (2) 20th December 1889 (3) Normanton	29th October 1889 Lawn Hill F.H. Hann	Witness. J.A. O'Shea	New South Wales all her life	(1) (2) (3)	
(1) C. A. Collard (2) 28th December 1889 (3) Normanton	27th December 1889 Normanton Cemetery William Jackson	Witnesses William R. Mills Herbert Holler	Normanton Queensland all her life	(1) (2) (3)	
(1) C. A. Collard. (2) [illegible] December 1889. (3) Normanton.	7th December 1889 Toowong Cemetery Brisbane W.G. Cowen	Witnesses. Jno H. Brown Charles Williams		(1) (2) (3)	
				(1) (2) (3)	

Normanton Police Quarters and plan including gaol below (NLA)

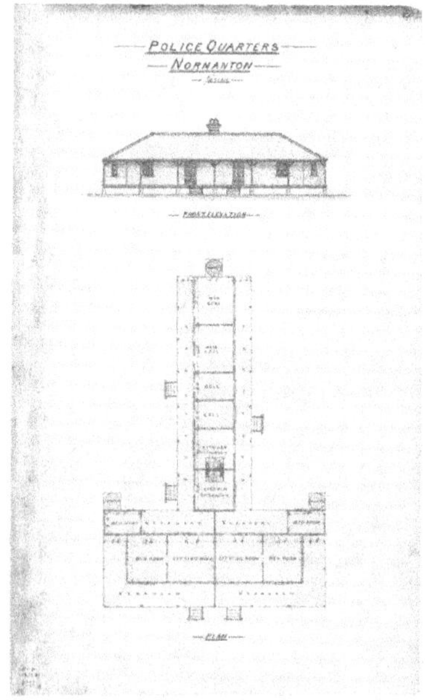

James Cashman in 1902. (SLQ)

Patrick Joseph Brannelly. (Queensland Police Museum)

Team of horses with a fully laden wagon, Inverleigh Station, 1908 (SLQ)

PJ Brannelly and Family (SLQ)

Lawn Hill Station (SLQ)

Judge TK Pater

Nym's Headstone

Port Darwin jetty with S.S. *Taiyuan* and *Catterthun*. Taken from Stokes Hill. (NT Library)

Fannie Bay Whipping Post (NT Library)

Robert Stott (SLSA)

Robert Stott (SLSA)

Turn off Lagoon Police Station (eHive)

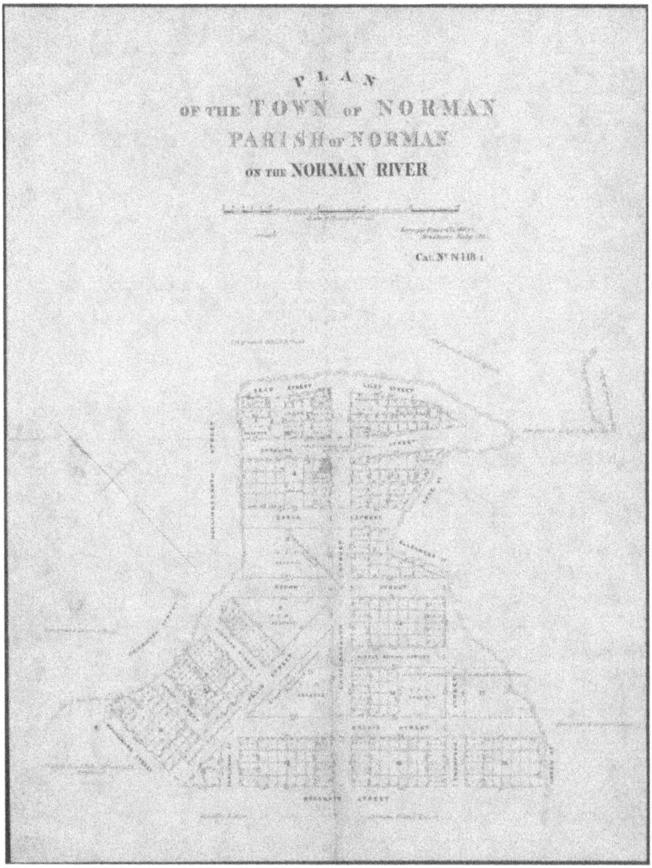

PLAN
OF THE TOWN OF NORMAN
PARISH OF NORMAN
ON THE NORMAN RIVER

Lawn Hill graves. Joe Flick at top left under water pipe frame. (Dick Eussen)

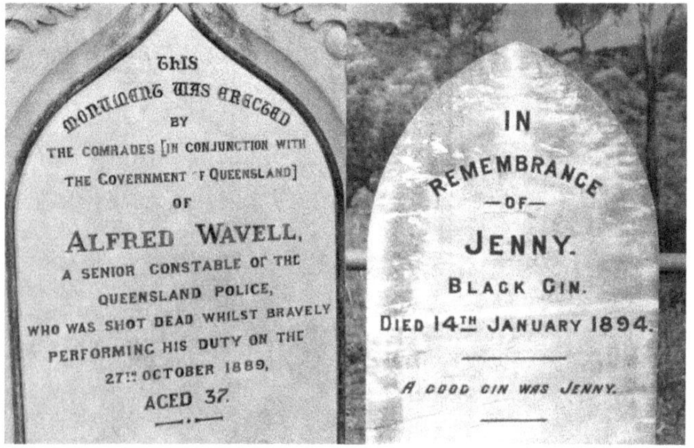

· CHAPTER 15 ·

Mary Theresa

JOE LED THE POLICE on the merriest dance of their lives. He walked backwards in his own footprints, swung from tree branches, and waded through waterholes. He stampeded police horses at night, sleeping only in snatches; enfolded by riverside tree trunks, or buried in a hollow under a creek bank.

Inspector Douglas and his men were canny enough to concentrate their efforts on the tracks heading west to the Territory. Knowing this, Joe hurried south along the Gregory River. Feinting in numerous directions, he stole two good horses from Armraynald Station, and rode both to a standstill as he set sail for Gregory Downs, with the police, realising their mistake, now in hot pursuit.

At the Gregory Hotel, the police hobbled out their plant and cut loose on a binge, while Joe lay under the floorboards of the front bar, listening to their drunken plans to 'teach that blasted Joe Flick a lesson.'

Bill Richardson, the Burketown to Camooweal mail man, was holding court on his favourite stool at the bar. He was known for a song and a smile and the yarns he picked up in his travels. Joe listened as the police threw back their heads and roared with laughter.

Later, he watched from the shadows as Richardson stripped to his undershorts and paid one of the hotel maids to wash his clothes, before heading off to bed. Not one to miss an opportunity, Joe waited until midnight, then snow-dropped the mail man's flannel shirts and dungarees from a clothes line. He also stole two horses, a saddle and a pack saddle belonging to the same man. The drunken slumber of the police party and hotel staff was so complete that Joe raided the kitchen for rations before heading off overland towards the Nicholson River.

The next day Richardson became a laughing stock when he appeared in the hotel bar wearing nothing but his undershorts, ranting and raving at the low beast of a man who had stolen his clothes.

This was too good a joke for the locals to resist, and his pleas to borrow new garb fell on deaf ears. Bill Richardson rode on to Burketown on a borrowed horse, in just a pair of white undershorts and a hat, becoming a Gulf legend in the process.

Joe was dry-camped on a ridge the following night when he heard a sound that spooked him. Silently he stole into the scrub, holding his breath. A moment later Monaghan Wilson stepped into the firelight, grinning widely as always.

'Where are ya Joe? Got no time for an ol' mate like me?'

Joe cracked a smile and hurried in to meet his friend, shaking his hand warmly. 'Ah, Monaghan, it's good to see you. How did you find me?'

'Easy, one of them ponies you nicked from old Bill Richardson is pigeon-toed. Any fool can track the bastard.'

'I'd best get rid of it then.'

'Yeah, let the bastard go, or they'll be on you soon enough.'

The two young men sat at the fire until the coals turned from red to pale orange, and light appeared in the eastern sky. They talked of things as if they were brothers, both on the wrong side of the law, but at home in the wilderness, on horseback and alone. The coming dawn meant that it was time to leave, and the two mates said farewell.

'Don't take them head-on, Joe,' Monaghan warned. 'Run again. Keep to the bush and they'll never find you.'

'Maybe,' said Joe. 'But I can't run forever, and I'll not let them capture me alive.'

When Monaghan left, the pigeon-toed horse trailed behind him from a lead. Joe's mate promised to release it on the Gregory, where the 'traps might follow those tracks to hell.'

Even with this ruse, however, by lunch time Joe climbed a rugged hillock on the plain and saw a cloud of dust that could only mean a gang of 'traps' in pursuit.

With a good breeze at his back, however, Joe put a packet of vestas he had taken from the Gregory Hotel to good use, dropping flaring matches into desiccated spear-grass, creating an inferno on a five-hundred-yard front hurtling away towards his pursuers, who had no choice but to escape into the nearby Blue Grass swamp to wait out the flames.

There, safe in muddy hollows, they battled mosquitoes, dysentery, and despondency. It was obvious that Joe was heading west now, and as the flames moved on, the police party dispersed, in need of rations and fresh horses. There was no way of tracking Joe through the newly burnt country.

Senior Constable Alfred Wavell, one of the best of those policemen, took his tracker, Trooper Garrie, and hurried back to their base at Turn-off Lagoon, unaware that he had just a few days left to live.

Meanwhile, still riding at break-neck pace, Joe reached the Nicholson, where he followed the main channel, still sluggish after the long dry season. He skirted the big waterhole at Bannockburn where, much later, Brethren missionaries would baptise souls from the relocated Doomadgee Mission.

At Corinda he released the horse that had borne him from the Gregory, for by then it was scarcely able to bear his weight. Nearby was the most northerly point of Lawn Hill Station, and home ground for Joe. Around here he knew every knoll and ant-hill studded plain, the swampy ground on the river bends where paperbarks matted the soil with their fibrous surface roots.

Without a weapon he had eaten only bush fruits, one turtle, and some emu eggs along the way. His hunger for meat was enough to send him into the scrub near Turn-off Lagoon, watching Tom Anderson's grog shanty, sniffing the air at the smell of cooking beef and vegetables, but there were too many people coming and going, loafers outside arguing and drinking. The police camp was also close by, making him wary.

Instead Joe moved on to the homestead owned by the Andersons. He watched from the gardens for a time: a couple of the house girls singing while they hung out washing, another playing with two young children, a boy and a girl, on a patch of green lawn.

When Joe saw Mrs Anderson walk down towards the river he followed her. In a white dress she looked clean and angelic to Joe, and she had always been nice to him.

To Joe's surprise, on the bank of the river she lifted her dress over her head, then slipped out of her underwear. Mrs Anderson was in her late twenties, and despite the children she had borne, she remained slim and pretty. Joe did not take his eyes away from her as she climbed into the water, washing and soaking in the effervescent pool.

It was a brave act to swim alone. Joe knew that 'gators were sometimes seen near here, though a barrage of lead generally accompanied any sighting. Not oblivious to the risks, she soon emerged, naked and dripping from the water. She had no towel, but dried off in the morning sun, singing softly to herself. Joe waited until she had dressed, and fixed her hair back in a complicated arrangement that seemed to include multiple pins.

Finally, as she turned to head back up to the house, Joe stepped from the shelter of the trees and stood watching her his face imploring her for help.

Mrs Anderson stopped dead still. 'Joe Flick, is that you?'

'Yes.'

'What are you doing here? They're looking for you everywhere.'

'I'm hungry for tucker, if you have anything.'

'Oh God, you poor thing … we can't tell Tom. Now listen to me, there's a tool shed just up behind the house, the small one. Go back and hide in there and I'll bring you some food.'

Later, Mrs Anderson came to the outhouse where he was hiding. A dog; a brindle-coloured beast of a thing, came with her, uttering a throaty growl when he saw Joe.

'Pet him a little, and he'll be friends with you,' she said.

Joe did as she suggested, nervously stroking the animal's head between his ears. The growling stopped and the dog moved to a corner where he settled down, laying his head on one paw, yellow eyes flickering open to watch Joe warily.

Mrs Anderson, for her part, hadn't experienced such excitement in a long time. Mary Theresa by name, she liked men and they liked her. Tom was her second husband, though he had not proved to be much more interesting than the first. In spite of that, she loved the lazily winding Nicholson and its pandanus-crowded banks, the homestead and her bevy of servants – much better than her home town of Forbes, in New South Wales, and her years with William Green in dry Eulo.

Mary Theresa passed Joe a plate heaped with beef, potatoes and gravy, then watched him eat.

'Did you like looking at me, when I was in the water, Joe?'

Joe shook his head. 'No Missus Anderson. I just wanted to talk to you. Because you've always been good to me.'

'Call me Mary, won't you please?'

'Yes, Mary,' Joe grinned, feeling content with the best meal he had eaten in months.

'Is there anything else you want?'

Joe decided to push his luck. She reminded him of a cat rubbing itself against the legs of its owner, purring and anxious to please. 'I need a gun. Can you get me one?'

The young woman felt a shock. This man was a fugitive, almost a bushranger, and she imagined what might happen down the track if she put a firearm in his hands.

Still, the next day she came back with a bundle wrapped in cloth. Inside, Joe found a revolver, along with two dozen caps, some powder, and bullets.

'It's one of Tom's old ones,' Maria said, 'but I know it works.'

Joe hefted it, examined the bore and spun the cylinder. 'Thank you.'

Meals came three times a day, and the activity was noticeable. The house girls, Joe noticed, started looking in his direction, and the gardener finally came close to the shed and looked inside.

Joe raised the revolver. 'Tell anyone I'm here and I'll kill you.'

The gardener ran away across the lawn. Joe knew he should leave that night, but he wanted to say goodbye to Mary, so he stayed.

It was a mistake. At dawn the next day one of the girls hurried to the outhouse, where Joe was enjoying an oatmeal porridge, dripping with molasses, that Mary had brought out for him.

'Missus say the p'lice are riding up. You'd better go.'

The warning gave Joe just enough time to take his revolver and head into the scrub, finding a vantage point with a view of the homestead drive. From there he watched Senior Constable Wavell and Trooper Garrie ride up. On foot beside them, lathered in sweat, was the gardener.

Mary came out to meet them, and her voice carried clearly to Joe. 'Why Constable Wavell, what brings you out here? A cup of tea?'

Wavell dipped his cap. 'Not just now, thank you. We've heard from your gardener here that the fugitive Joe Flick was seen near the house.'

Mary was unflustered. 'Well he's mistaken.' She shot a disapproving look at the gardener. 'There was one light-skinned boy who came and asked for work a day or two back and I gave him a feed, but it wasn't Yella Joe. I'd know him a mile off, seen him lots of times before.'

'Can we have a look around?' asked Wavell.

'Of course you can. Go wherever you like.'

After listening to every word, Joe turned, and careful not to leave any sign, headed down to the river.

That night, Wavell ate dinner at the grog shanty, on the verandah. Trooper Garrie was not welcome in the dining room itself, but he was tolerated under the bough-shaded awning. Joe saw that their mounts were tethered out the front.

This was an opportunity too good to ignore. He knew exactly where the police horse paddock was. It was time to get himself a new mount, and sabotage any efforts to catch him in the process.

Hurrying across country, it was still light when Joe came upon the post and rail fence that marked the beginning of the police paddock. Ten, maybe a dozen horses were grazing peacefully.

Joe waited for full darkness, then mustered all the horses, including one he knew was called Collector, and another handy looking bay. The latter he tacked up with a saddle he found on a rail. With the pistol in his belt, he drove the small mob out towards the track, finally waking the sleeping man who shouted after him and ran for his rifle.

It would have been easy enough to ride away from there, perhaps head for the Territory border again, but Joe did not intend to run so far from home. He drove the mob of police horses at a canter back to the Turn-off Lagoon shanty, rousing all and sundry as he passed along the route. Men and women alike emerged from wurlies, humpies and tents, or stood from camp fires to see the commotion passing by.

Joe let the mob mill in confusion outside Anderson's grog shanty, shielding himself with a cloud of dust. In an act of utter bravado he paused to untie and lead away the policemen's mounts while they were still drinking and eating inside. One was a well-known and indefatigable police mount with the unlikely name of Railway.

'Yah,' shouted Joe, whirling in that maelstrom, waving the revolver in his right hand while the raucous drinkers shouted and the policemen dropped their forks and tumblers to see, drawing their revolvers as they came. But the front of the pub was confused with running horses and a lone rider who moved so fast that no one could hope to shoot him.

Taking control of the mob, Joe drove them from town, safe in the knowledge that the police would need to procure new mounts before they could follow, and that they were unlikely to go after an armed man in the night.

On the way out of town Joe steeled himself for what he knew he must do to slow down any pursuit. Two miles out, he rounded the police horses into a set of disused yards. Dismounting, he methodically shot all but two in the head with his revolver. They fell like bags of sand to the dirt, kicked a few times while the others shied and whinnied at the sound and smells of death.

Then, mounted on the bay, and with another as a spare, Joe set off for his homelands: the Lawn Hill country that made his heart beat with longing.

· CHAPTER 16 ·

On Joe's Trail

THE NEXT MORNING, BEFORE dawn, Senior Constable Alfred Wavell lit a slush lantern and sat down at his desk at the Turn-off Lagoon Police Station. He had been up during the night, forced out of bed by a bout of dysentery.

The necessity of finding new horses and setting out after Joe Flick was a heavy weight on Alfred's shoulders. He knew that dire consequences were coming, one way or another.

Inking a fresh quill, he wrote a letter to his mother, Harriet Wavell, far away on the Isle of Wight. Once this was done he prepared a last will and testament, leaving everything he owned to his widowed sister.

At thirty-eight years Alfred was no longer feeling young, and with his recent illness he'd been wondering if he might soon return to the green fields and dramatic cliffs of home, before he grew too old to make a meaningful start there.

Alfred had been a member of the Queensland Police Force on and off since 1872, a career that was besmirched by charges against him, first for 'boarding in a public house,' and soon after 'having married a prostitute against the advice of his superiors.' This second offence led to Alfred being dismissed from the service. Competent, popular police officers were not easy to find, however, and by 1882 he held the position of camp-keeper at Normanton, with the badge number of 488. In 1888 he accepted a promotion to Senior Constable in charge at Turn-off Lagoon.

When the letter and document were done, Alfred wrote in the station journal that he was about to set off after Joe Flick: 'I am determined to apprehend Flick at all costs, and will not leave the outlaw's tracks until he is in our custody.'

This done, Alfred instructed Trooper Garrie to ready their packs and firearms. They then faced the embarrassing task of walking to the Andersons, there to borrow horses to replace those that Joe Flick had taken.

Mary answered the door, a worried expression on her face. 'Oh it's you, Alfred. Please be careful … I had a terrible dream about you last night ... that Joe Flick shot you dead.'

Wavell tried to shrug it off, 'Lucky for me dreams aren't mortal.'

'I mean it. Be careful … I heard what happened last night. Take all the horses you need, and Godspeed.'

As the police party was about to leave, with nine good horses haltered on the roadway, Alfred bid Mary farewell on the verandah.

'We appreciate the horses, but please, tell me something. You knew that it was Joe Flick hanging around here. Why didn't you tell us?'

Mary Theresa's skin turned white and her lips pursed with shock. 'That's a lie.'

Alfred stared her down. He saw many things in that woman's face and he didn't like any of them.

Within an hour they were on the track, heading downstream. Garrie easily followed the sign made by Joe's mob of stolen horses as he left town the previous evening. Two miles out they found the old yards and the fallen, bloodied equine corpses, attended by a cloud of flies that must have numbered in the millions, collectively making a row like a locomotive. Alfred felt sick as he walked that bloodstained ground. Several of the horses had been his, and highly valued they were too.

'What kind of man would do this?' Alfred wondered aloud, and the clenched knot of dysentery in his gut was writhing, combining with the strength of this horror at the dangers that might face them when they found Joe Flick.

Tracking from that point onwards was not easy, for the humidity and heat were building, leaving a film of sweat that soaked shirts and ran down over eyes. Besides, Joe Flick was in his element. At one stage, Garrie became confused, and they made no progress, until the tracker discerned that the outlaw had bound sheaves of grass to his horses' hooves in an effort to obscure their tracks. Only the keenest of eyes and attention to detail allowed Garrie to follow a trail of broken stalks, that a lesser observer would never have noticed.

Very early the next morning they reached Bannockburn, where they found that the manager, a man called Symes, had been up half the night, frantic with worry after a horseman had ridden close-up in the night, and pelted the place with stones. The stone-throwing had stopped only when Symes fetched his rifle.

'It must have been Joe Flick,' said Alfred. 'He's angry now.'

Garrie inclined his head sagely, for he could read anger in a man's tracks as if it were written on a page.

Nearby, at the Bannockburn police horse paddock, they selected fresh horses, and met with Constable Gunn. The two white policemen drank tea, and Gunn loaned Alfred another tracker, Trooper Noble.

Noble was named for his looks – tall and regal. Born on the Statton River near Kowanyama, he was a crack shot, and one of the best trackers Alfred had worked with.

Joe's tracks now led them southwards, to the headwaters of the Widdallion in the rugged Edith Range. This was wild country, and hard work for the trackers. Later that day, however, Alfred was considering a quick dinner stop, when there came a shout from some hundred paces ahead. 'Boss, boss, there he is, Joe Flick!'

Wavell touched his spurs to his horse and charged off the back legs, heedless of deep holes and wayward paperbark trunks. He could hear Noble doing the same on his flank. The riverine brush swept by his face and adrenalin flooded his system.

Ahead they saw Joe, mounted up on the near bank, turning his horse to face them, then rearing up with an angry shout, waving his pistol. The creek was a sheet of vivid blue, dotted with lily-pads, and fringed with gravel sands.

'Stop there,' Joe shouted. 'Go back home. Follow me no more.'

Wavell took his horse forward, rifle held low, ready to fire from the hip. 'Give up, Joe Flick. You can't take on the British Empire.'

Joe's face was a mask of fury as he raised his weapon and fired once into the air, the echoes clattering and birds taking to the wing from all along the creek. Before Alfred could respond Joe urged his horse into the water, churning the surface into foam. The three policemen peppered the air with lead, accompanied by clouds of powder smoke, but Joe was by then on the other side and galloping away.

Noble and Garrie took up the pursuit, while Alfred rode into Joe's camp, where a smouldering fire and almost-cooked johnny-cakes told the story. A welcome sight was a horse tied to a branch of a she-oak.

'Well if it isn't my old boy Collector,' said Alfred, dismounting. The roan gelding was one of his favourite horses, and he was pleased to add him to the train, despite his wasted condition.

By the time he had crossed the creek, Noble and Garrie were on their way back, having lost sight of their quarry, ready for a horse change and shaking their heads at how Joe Flick rides like the wind itself down gullies and through scrub as if they were made of thin air.

Yet it would be dogged persistence, not speed, Alfred knew, that would win the day, and Garrie was already on the spoor, leading them southwards along that picturesque waterway, cut through slabs of yellow-orange stone; a world of rock, water and sky.

They found another abandoned horse, ridden almost into the ground. Nearby were signs that showed how Joe had stumbled on a small mob of station brumbies and cut one out. Only the most skilled and desperate horseman would attempt to break and ride a mount on the run. That's what Joe had done.

The tracks showed how close he came to being bucked off, but Joe somehow seemed to have kept his seat. Garrie shook his head in wonder. 'That horse pig-root long time here. That bloke never fall.'

On stony ground, even Garrie could not follow unshod horse tracks and the process became more guess-work than certainty. Still, they rode on at snail's pace into the evening, when a build-up season storm began to flicker and rumble on the horizon.

'It's getting too dark for tracking in this country,' said Alfred, 'and the lightning doesn't help. My guess is that Joe's heading for Lawn Hill Homestead. It might be best now to get there first and stop any mischief that he might be planning.'

Yet, on that long night ride, dysentery again tightened its grip. Alfred had to stop many times, and he was so weak that he tied himself to the saddle as a precaution. The tracking of Joe Flick seemed to be an ordeal without end.

Kitty told me how that night she was sleeping next to Henry in their camp at the silver mine, of how the night was dark apart from the storm clouds throwing lightning bolts to the earth like bullets. She related how they heard an unearthly wail from out in the night, the sound of weeping so terrible it tore at her heart.

She told me how she gripped Henry's shoulder, and sobbed. 'Oh mercy, it's Joe. He's out there.'

She told me how the pair of them went out of the hut, where coals from the cooking hearth-fire glowed hellish orange. Of how they heard the sound of a horse's hooves moving skittishly out in the scrub, as if the rider had reached an impassable but imaginary barrier.

'Mother,' cried the voice, unearthly, low, but unmistakeable.

'Joe,' cried Kitty, 'my son. Come in to us, please do.'

In reply came the sound of more weeping; great sobs and wails that rose and fell through the night winding around the white trunks of gums and the stones and mullock heaps of the mine.

'I'm sorry … forgive me,' Joe went on. 'For what I done … for what I know I will do.'

'Come to us, boy,' said Henry. 'It's not too late.'

More weeping then, and those same sideways movements of the horse. 'I can't. Forgive me …'

'Please Joe,' wailed Kitty.

'Good bye,' Joe cried.

Then, accompanied by the sound of hoof beats, he rode away from her for the last time.

The next morning, just in time for breakfast, Senior Constable Wavell, along with Troopers Noble and Garrie, saw the flat-topped mount that gave Lawn Hill its name. They rode up to the homestead, relieved to see no signs of trouble.

A group of people, including a ringer called Bird, and a visitor from nearby Riversleigh Station, Robert Doyle, were sitting down to breakfast in the outbuilding that served as a dining room. Frank Hann himself was out on the run 'dealing with' some horse-spearing Waanyi.

'We need rations,' Alfred cried to the Chinese cook, 'and breakfast too, as fast as you can manage.' Even though he was having trouble keeping food in his system, Alfred knew that he required the sustenance. He joined the others at the table. Garrie and Noble ate outside.

They had just finished eating, waiting for another cup of tea when beautiful dark Opal, one of the station concubines, arrived at the door, telling them breathlessly that she had just seen Joe Flick trying to catch a horse in the house paddock. Wavell stood and grabbed his rifle. Within a moment he was out the door, calling for his men.

'The escaped prisoner is here,' cried Alfred. 'And justice, at last, is nigh.'

· CHAPTER 17 ·

The Battle of Lawn Hill

ONE EARLY MORNING IN the beginning of April I rose, left the bunk house and headed outside. The Gulf waters were mirror-calm in the distance and the air felt drier and cooler than it had in all the months since my arrival. As I walked, listening to the chatter of a pair of blue-wing kookaburras in the carbeen trees, I was surprised to see Kitty waiting for me. She was carrying a dilly bag with some tucker and a canvas water bag that looked like it had seen better days.

I walked across to greet her. 'Hello Kitty, you're up here early.'

Grunting a low greeting she turned her pearl-shell eyes away. 'Might be you an' me go drive in your car,' she said. It wasn't really a question.

I was surprised. I had plans for the day, and my little Riley motor car had not travelled more than five miles since I arrived at the mission. 'Where do you want to go?'

'Three, maybe four days out bush, all up. No more.'

'I guess we can, if you want to. Will you give me an hour to get ready?'

Kitty nodded, and sat down on the grass. She had her pipe out, but looked around carefully before she lit up. The Brethren missionaries had a thing about women smoking, though they didn't seem to mind the same activity being practised by the men.

While Kitty smoked I cleared the trip with Len Akehurst, cadged a full tank of fuel and a couple of jerricans, then packed the gear I'd need for a few nights of sleeping rough. Dorothy gave me a box of rations for the trip, and tutted at my frustration at not knowing the destination for our journey.

'Feel privileged,' she said. 'Old Kitty trusts you, and after the things she's been through, that's a wondrous thing.'

We drove out, dodging bog-holes still treacherous from the wet season. After an intrepid day's travel, talking only intermittently, we camped the first night on the banks of the Nicholson River. At bed-time I stretched out on the back seat of the car and Kitty curled up beside the fire, snoring softly as she slept.

The next day we forded the river at Corinda, and followed trails that were worse still than those of the previous day, crawling along a bridle track through stations with names that remain implanted on my memory: Merton Vale, Hinton, Lochinvar and Lincoln. Kitty directed me with sharp commands, showing a sense of direction that was uncanny in a world of twisted scrub, dry waving spear-grass and termite hills.

Eventually we came up to a place from which we could see the complex of buildings around the Lawn Hill Station homestead. We saw men, dust, a motor truck, and someone bringing a mob of horses into the yards. Kitty asked me to stop the car.

Sitting cross-legged on the dry grass, she began to cry, fat drops falling from her eyes, and a low, throaty keening sound emanating from deep down in her chest.

The twenty-seventh of October, in the year 1889, was a fateful day in the history of Queensland's North. Telegrams of alarm were crossing the vast and lonely outback spaces, with the Commissioner himself instructing Inspector Douglas to 'go out with any available men, and capture the desperado at all hazards.'

Joe Flick had been awake all night, and now lurked restlessly on the fringes of the station's home paddock, waiting for an opportunity to replace the magnificent but wild horse that had fought him every step through the dark hours. Tired of running, Joe was filled with a burning anxiety.

The great gorges of Lawn Hill were mere miles away now. In that wilderness, Joe knew that he could hide from the police forever. After a childhood spent roaming the area he knew every pool, every cranny of rock. But the revolver Mary Theresa had given him had only four caps left, and scarcely enough powder for three rounds. He needed weapons, and rations.

Watching Wavell's party of police arrive and head into the station, Joe knew that he had to act. He waited until they were in the mess eating breakfast before opening a wire gate and riding in. There were plenty of good mounts there, some of which he remembered from doing stock work for Frank Hann.

Dismounting, Joe had the saddle and bridle off in a moment. Carrying both, he approached one of the station horses, yet when he took a step forward the animal whinnied and backed away.

'Come on boy,' he said, forcing himself to relax, clicking his tongue and talking quietly. Reassured, the gelding allowed him to come close, at which point Joe put the saddle on the ground. After gently petting the horse's neck he slipped his right forearm around the off side of its head, effortlessly sliding the bit between its teeth with his left hand, then adjusting the crown over his ears. The saddle followed, all very quickly done, and without alarming the horse.

Joe had just tightened the girth and mounted up when an armed contingent reined in at the top of the rise. Two Native Police troopers began to walk their horses down towards him, rifles extended.

Joe cried 'Yah,' and dug in his heels. Within ten paces he was galloping at full tilt, the humid-hot air on his face, and dirt flying from pounding hooves.

Taking a fateful decision he rode not away from the troopers, but towards them, splitting them neatly.

The first shot directed towards Joe disrupted the air around his ears, yet he did not flinch. Headed directly towards the homestead now, he jumped a fence and bypassed the armed party, a move they had not expected.

Bullets, however, fly faster than a man can ride. Whipping and cracking through the air, one soon found its mark, taking Joe's new mount in the chest and bringing him down in a tumbled heap. Joe freed his feet from the stirrups, then sprinted for the nearest of the outbuildings.

'Shoot him,' Alfred Wavell cried from the saddle, his voice carrying clearly. 'Now's the time, boys. Bring him down.'

Joe, however, was fast and elusive, soon reaching the relative safety of a small bark-clad hut. The door was closed but unlocked. He twisted the handle and shoved with his shoulder. Inside were stacked bags of lime and cement, heavy iron tools and some old harness. No weapons. Joe swore to himself, and hurried out the way he had come.

Looking around the corner to see the police dismounting and preparing to follow, Joe ran for the next building, a substantial structure with galvanised iron walls and shuttered windows – an old dining room that now served as a bunkhouse for the head stockman. Pulling open the door, he hurried inside, eyes adjusting to the relative dark. Rummaging in and around a cupboard, he located a modern Colt revolver. Mounted on a gun rack he found a Greener choke-bore shotgun. Cartridges for both firearms were on a shelf.

Feeling more positive now, Joe barricaded himself inside the hut, forcing a table against the door. After loading both shotgun and revolver he partially opened a turret-like window shutter. From surreptitious movement and the sound of furtive voices he realised that the police and their allies were now behind cover nearby.

Joe glared out the window, sweat dripping from his hair and coating his wiry arms. The gun felt good in his hands, the forestock resting on the window sill.

Five minutes passed, then a voice called: 'Joe Flick, listen to me.'

The words came from behind the station store.

'My name is Senior Constable Alfred Wavell. I want to talk.'

'Go on then,' yelled Joe. 'Talk.'

Wavell showed himself, walking out from behind the store and slowly coming closer. His revolver was in its holster, and he carried no other weapon. 'Surrender now,' the policeman said. 'We have armed men on all sides. Walk out of the building with your hands up or face the consequences.'

Wavell had made a fatal mistake. Whether it was the dysentery affecting his mind, or just a moment of carelessness, he came too close. Too far from cover. Too late to run. Most fatefully of all, he had misjudged Joe Flick's state-of-mind.

Joe sighted on Alfred Wavell's chest, and held his aim despite the trembling inside. The years of being called Yella Joe and counted as something less than a man; the months of running; the taunts; the gunshot wound in the back; the sixteen court appearances in Palmerston, and the way that they had tricked him into thinking that he had been released, all built to a pure and deadly rage.

In an instant of time that could never be taken back, Joe squeezed the trigger and the tightly-packed charge of pellets struck Wavell in the chest. The policeman reacted with that strange little leap of a heart-shot animal, then crumpled without a cry and barely a tremble.

Joe felt a great calmness descend on him as he watched the policeman's blood stain the earth, and listened to the horrified exclamations of the men still hidden behind the outbuildings.

No one came out to try to take Alfred's body. He lay there, mourned only by clouds of flies and shrouded in heat, a long way from his mother and his birthplace on the Isle of Wight.

For a long time Joe was left to his own thoughts and the ravages of his conscience. Fittingly, that afternoon, a storm swept in, darkening the sky and smelling of sweet rain after the terrible heat of the day. It brought deep rumbles and white lightning from clouds blacker than pitch.

Frank Hann rode back from a day of 'dispersing' blacks with blood on his shoes and a Martini-Henry rifle in his hand. A bandolier of cartridges hung diagonally from one shoulder, over his usual Crimean shirt. His tracker Nym and a stockman called O'Shea rode with him.

Opal met Hann at the house fence, flinging her arms around him as soon as he had dismounted.

'Murder, murder,' she cried. 'There's been murder done here this day.'

'Was it Joe Flick that done it?'

'Yes, it was Joe.'

'Who did he kill?'

'Constable Wavell.'

'Damn him,' Hann snorted. 'How did it come to this?'

Hann gave Opal his horse to see to, and conferred with Robert Doyle, listening to the story grimly before walking around the side of the store. There he saw Wavell's body still lying where it had fallen, on the ground near the old dining room, in the light rain that had just started to patter on the roofs of the station buildings.

The station owner turned back to address the two troopers, Noble and Garrie. 'Hadn't any of you the gumption to fetch in Alfred's body? Shame on you.'

Still holding his loaded rifle, Hann walked out in the open. He was not a big man but he prided himself on his pluck. 'Joey,' he called, 'don't shoot. You know I've not done you a wrong turn in all my days.'

'Go back, Mr Hann,' cried Joe.

'For the love of God, why did you do it, Joey? Come out of there now.'

'I won't come out.'

Hann walked to Wavell's body, squatted beside it, and examined the wound. 'It's a terrible thing you've done, Joey.'

'If I hadn't shot Wavell he would have shot me,' Joe said, his voice almost breaking with the strain. 'And if I surrender now they'll hang me.'

Hann stood up again. 'That's true enough, but there's a chance that if you give up without further bloodshed the judge will look kindly on it.'

'Perhaps,' Joe said, 'you might be right.' Then, in a whisper, 'Yet I lived my life saying yes sir and no sir, and taking kicks and slaps from men like you. Could you promise me that they won't clap irons on me? I swore I wouldn't let that happen again.'

Mistakenly taking this as some kind of promise, Frank Hann walked around to the front door of the hut, and pushed it open, forcing back the table barricade. As the door swung open, and in a flash of lightning, Hann saw Joe's sweating face, and the tense muscles of his hands holding a revolver. Then came a heavy boom, and a muzzle flash. The ball struck Hann's chest and passed out between his shoulder blades.

Hann fell to his knees, raising his Martini Henry at the same time. He fired once, though the bullet went astray. Bleeding badly and afraid that the killing shot would come next, Hann staggered back to where Doyle remained behind cover. The older man took off his shirt and used it to bind the wound.

'The treacherous snake,' Doyle swore.

Almost sick with pain, Hann sagged against a wall, sorely hit. 'Fire on him. Kill him. Joe Flick has gone to the devil now.'

· CHAPTER 18 ·

Joe's Last Stand

TROOPERS GARRIE AND NOBLE, along with Doyle, O'Shea and Bird, fired their weapons into the galvanised iron sides of the hut until it was peppered with holes. The senior policeman was dead, and Hann was bandaged up in bed, so Robert Doyle placed himself in charge of the effort to end the bloody siege. He was a hard man himself, spending six months of each year on the road droving cattle, and a natural leader.

When two handy local cattlemen, Harry Shadforth and Dan Carlyon rode in, Doyle felt that they had enough manpower on hand to ask Bird to mount up and ride to Burketown for assistance.

Still the firing went on. It sounded like a battle, with booming discharges and clouds of powder smoke. Now and then, a window shutter would ease open and Joe Flick fire off a shot with revolver or shotgun. Towards dark the cloud cover thickened, and heavier rain began to fall.

Inside the bunkhouse, Joe understood that the police were no longer interested in taking him alive. With the station and its ample store of ammunition at their disposal, they used cartridges like water, while Joe could scarcely see a target worthy of the name. He piled more furniture against the doors and windows, for he knew the penetrative power of modern projectiles. Over the following hours he flinched each time the police slugs crashed and whined through the walls and inside. The floor was by then littered with flattened lumps and flakes of lead, along with spent cartridge cases from Joe's return fire.

A ricocheting projectile glanced off the point of Joe's ankle, and he howled with pain. The bullet shattered the bone, and damaged nerves behind it. With the wound wrapped tightly, he could only just manage to stand on his feet, wincing and hissing with pain as he did so. Meanwhile thunder cracked and rain hammered on the roof.

Around midnight a .577 calibre Snider bullet smashed its way through the wall. It ploughed through one side of Joe's stomach and out the other, opening an ugly wound. Blood flowed through jagged slits in his skin, and set off a deep pain, as if some terrible creature had taken up residence in his gut.

Sobbing in the darkness, Joe staunched the flow as best he could, using some kerchiefs he found in a valise. Unwilling to believe that he was mortally hit, he decided that if he was to hold the police off, and have any chance to escape into the wild Lawn Hill gorge country to heal his wounds, he had to leave now.

Soon after, when the rain was heaviest, and fearing that the police might storm the hut, Joe pushed open the door, looked around for activity, then crawled away from the darkened buildings, moving towards the escarpment that led down to the creek.

This broken slope was difficult to manage in the rain, with mud running between the stones and his legs slick with blood. His hands gripped roots and the stiff stalks of small shrubs. The shotgun, slung over his back, and supply of cartridges slowed him down. Lightning lit his way, and his breath hacked in and out of his lungs. His eyes crinkled tightly against the pain that made frontal assaults on his senses.

Over an hour of effort, Joe made it down to the creek, heading to the water to clean his wounds and drink. By the time dawn arrived he had made it only five or six hundred yards southwards along the creek. Soon the trackers would be on his trail, Joe knew, and he was close to the limit of his strength.

Crawling through thick spear and kangaroo grass, he stopped between two huge paperbark trunks, shielded from view by green pandanus fronds. There, Joe decided, he could make a stand, and perhaps, he told himself, hold them off and get away.

That morning, bandaged and sore, Frank Hann impressed everyone by insisting that he rise, dress, and join the action. When Rob Doyle led an early morning rush into the hut Joe had occupied, Hann limped along in the rear of the party. They found the floor covered in smeared blood stains and spread with spent cases.

'Joey's hit bad,' said Hann. 'He must be close to finished.'

After a hearty breakfast, Hann took command back from his neighbour, splitting the company into two. One group would dig Alfred Wavell's grave, the other start tracking Joe.

Soon after, Joe Flick watched the wounded Hann, O'Shea, and Rob Doyle carry Wavell's body down from the homestead area and select a site not more than a hundred yards away from his hiding place. Of course, Joe understood that they would bury the dead constable on the riverbank, for the rocky ground around the homestead would have been too hard to dig the required six feet down. He felt sorry to see the sheet-wrapped corpse with its blood stains, but was too far gone to truly know remorse.

He had not slept beyond short naps since he left Mary Theresa's shed, and lost more blood than his body could regenerate. His hands shook on the shotgun stock, and his eyes were bleary.

A second party soon came into view, descending the steep ground down from the homestead, following Joe's trail. He recognised Troopers Noble and Garrie, Hann's boy Nym, and Harry Shadforth. Of course, even with the rain, Joe's route was easy to follow, and the men shouted with excitement at each new sighting of a mark where a foot had slid, or the deep red pigment of Joe's blood on a stone.

The tracking party continued past where their mates were digging Wavell's grave, then walked on towards Joe, as tense as soldiers, rifles loaded and ready, studying the ground as they came. Trooper Garrie found the place where Joe had gone to the water's edge, and then where he had left it again.

It was the station 'boy' Nym, with his sharp eyes, who looked ahead and saw Joe's shotgun barrel amongst the pandanus fronds.

'Look out,' he cried, pointing. 'There's Joe Flick now.'

Joe took steady aim at Nym's chest, and fired. The choke-bore shotgun thumped against his shoulder and Nym went down. The other members of the party, including the gravediggers, fell into cover like skittles.

Despite being struck in the chest by a charge of pellets, the range was long, and Nym did not die quickly. He twitched and thumped, and cried out. His feet galloped as if in an imaginary foot race. Frank Hann made a sound, a bellowing cry of rage, and crawled to the dying man, cradling him in his arms and comforting him with soft, crooning words until Nym finally fell silent.

The police contingent responded to Nym's death with a barrage of gunfire. Joe let go of the shotgun and brought up his revolver. As he extended his arm and squeezed off a shot, a bullet struck him in the upper leg, and another grazed across the side of his chest.

By the middle of the afternoon Joe was passing in and out of consciousness. He fought death like a warrior, but apart from one half-hearted charge by Trooper Noble, still the police party would not rush him. Instead they raised hats on sticks to tempt Joe to use his ammunition. He obliged by riddling them with gunfire. He was desperate for the coming of another night, still believing that he would crawl away and escape.

The next tactic, suggested by Trooper Noble, and ordered by Frank Hann, was the lighting up of the grass. Joe watched them circle upwind and drop burning matches at intervals. He emptied all six chambers of his revolver towards them.

After some initial success, the fire did not take well in the wet grass. It burned fitfully, yet streamed acrid smoke so Joe could scarcely breathe. More bullets came. One struck Joe high up in the skull. It felt just like the impact of a hammer, but it was the stomach wound that was slowly strangling the life out of him.

Not long after sunset, having lost all function in his gut, and having bled almost dry, Joe fired his last, despairing shot across the partially burned ground.

A few hours later, during the night; alone, frightened, crying with pain, but still dreaming of the gorge country and a life of freedom, the last living breath slipped from Joe Flick's lips and he died where he lay.

All night the police party kept watch, firing into the pandanus at intervals, but no one was willing to risk going close in the darkness.

'Surely he's dead,' grumbled Hann, whose wound was bleeding and becoming more painful. But no individual could be persuaded to go in after Joe. After all, he had killed two men and wounded another. No one wanted to be next.

A little after sunrise, however, Hann clapped Trooper Garrie on the back. 'For God's sake now. Go in and see.'

Garrie loped forward, holding his loaded Snider rifle at the balance point. Shadforth and Noble followed close behind.

Reaching the pandanus clump, they all watched Garrie lean forward, lift the rifle to his shoulder, then fire into Joe's head 'just to make sure.'

'Joe Flick is properly dead, boss,' reported Garrie, waving his rifle like a flag.

'Of course he is,' said Hann, limping forward with a grin on his face. 'I told you as much and we've been sitting here all night for no reason.'

More shouts of excitement now and the white men competed to be first to reach Joe's body. They dragged him out of the pandanus by the heels, and laid him in the open near where Wavell's grave was now being finished.

Joe wore no shirt, only trousers, though dried blood covered his trunk and arms. His body was marked with between nine and fourteen gunshot wounds, and his forehead was caved in as if from a sledgehammer. The exact number of rounds he had taken was unclear, as there was much argument about entry and exit points.

When Kitty and Henry Flick arrived at the creek, the men in the party were busy digging two more graves: one for Joe Flick next to Wavell, and another for Nym, some distance back towards the homestead. The conquering heroes took turns on the shovels while the others souvenired spent cartridges, items from Joe's pockets and even locks of his hair.

Kitty saw her son's bloody wounds, his thin body without any trace of fat, as lean as a goanna. She cried out and wailed, fell and smashed her face to the ground. Her fingers grasped a sharp stick and with this she drew a bloody trail down between her breasts.

'Get the gin away,' growled Doyle, and they took Kitty far enough away that all she could do was watch as they lifted Joe, ready to drop him into his grave.

'Plant him facing hell, boys,' cried Hann. 'Speed his way to the devil.'

And that was what they did. They buried Joe Flick face-down. Two of the men hawked and spat on his back before the first shovelful of earth went in.

Kitty told me how Trooper Noble was visibly shaken from the sight of the body, and seemed ashamed, almost horrified at what he had done. He sat on the ground away from the others, by himself with his head in his hands, his stripped-off police jacket and rifle lying abandoned on the dirt beside him.

Later, when Rob Doyle headed home to Riversleigh, Noble went with him, swearing that he would never carry a gun for white men again.

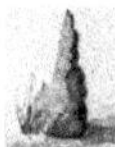

When Kitty had finished telling me the story, she took me down to the creek below the homestead. We first passed two graves, one for a house 'girl' called Jenny, the second for the 'boy,' Nym. Some distance to the west, towards the creek, we found a headstone dedicated to Wavell, and beside it a mound of clay where no grass or flowers grew, marking the final resting place of Joe himself.

Kitty was silent by then, her eyes as old as stone. I walked to the creek bank and stared at the pale green water, with its archer fish and tiny insects, the heads of little crocodiles hunting fish out in the steam. My hands were opening and closing, wishing I had a weapon. I wanted to avenge Joe. I wanted blood. But the men who killed him were just spirits and ghosts. And of course I felt sorry also, for Nym and Alfred

Wavell, who Joe had murdered. They were victims too, caught in the crossfire of Joe's circumstances.

I sat down there, on the bloodstained bank of that creek, and waited until Kitty was ready to go home.

CHAPTER 19

Epilogue

THESE PAGES DIM WITH my tears as I attempt to record what happened next, as if the death of Joe was not enough for the Flick family to endure.

Less than two years after the death of Joe, Kitty rode into Turn-off Lagoon for supplies. A man called Tom Perry, manager of Creswell Downs Station, passing through on his way back to the Territory, took a fancy to her. Fresh from an all-day drinking session at Anderson's shanty he blocked her way as she tried to walk into the store.

'Well hello there,' he said. 'How about you come on home with me, an' warm me swag? I got plenny tucker. Plenny tabacker.'

'No,' said Kitty, backing away, then turning to run, heading for her own horse. Perry mounted up and galloped to block her off, as if she were a calf trying to run from the mob. With that avenue of escape closed to her, Kitty ran for the scrub around the waterhole.

Chasing her down on horseback, Perry struck her to the ground with a stirrup iron. Later, he cuffed her to his saddle Ds, forcing her to walk and run alongside as he took her up the wild Nicholson and across the border into the Territory.

Henry Flick was furious when he heard, and swore that he would get Kitty back. Now Henry was not a good man. He had abducted many women himself over the years. Each had, for a time, shared his bed in preference to Joe's mother, and some had become pregnant with his children. It was partly a sense of pride and property that made him go after Kitty, and partly his genuine feelings for her.

Since Joe's death, Henry was no longer working. He was in a poor financial state. He outfitted his rescue mission by stealing horses, tack and rations from Frank Hann at Lawn Hill. Thus prepared, he set off in pursuit, in the heat of the build-up season.

The Hedley Track was notorious for taking lives when things went wrong.

German-born Henry Flick, son of a vine dresser and father of an outlaw, died of dehydration and heat exhaustion near Cresswell Creek, Northern Territory. The police later found his body twisted and wracked from the pain and distress of his last hours. His rifle was still gripped in his hands in testament to what he might have done to Tom Perry if he had reached him alive.

As for Kitty herself, she remained enslaved by Tom Perry for several years. His full name was Thomas Augustus Perry, a nephew of the great mariner John Lort Stokes. Perry's appetite for black women was legendary, and there were several attempts on his life by angry husbands. He was eventually shot and killed at the Bowgan outstation, by an unknown assassin who fired into his hut from the doorway.

I sometimes fancied that it was Kitty herself who pulled the trigger. May God forgive me, but I hope that she did. I can almost picture the deep brown pools of her eyes as she fired the round that sent Perry slumping to the floor in a puddle of his own rapacious blood.

But then, as happens with all of us, Kitty began to age. Strangers no longer wanted her. This was a relief to Kitty. For thirty years she drifted, sometimes to the blacks' camp at Lawn Hill where she could be close to her son's grave. Then to Burketown, and finally the mission at Old Doomadgee, where our talks began. She stayed only a little longer than I, however. Not a year after I left, a cyclone destroyed the mission, and the facility was removed to the Nicholson River, where New Doomadgee remains to this day.

Sadly, years of mission work had taken their toll on Len Akehurst. He went into retirement back in Sydney, ill from recurring malaria, boils, and headaches. He fought demons in his mind that he never fully escaped.

Len's successor, Mel Read, wrote to me a year or two after the move to inform me that Kitty had died. I wept for her one last time, and never forgot her, not even when I fought my battles in North Africa. After the war I had a strong desire to put my notes and jottings together into a readable format but could not summon the strength to do so.

Kitty's story had touched my heart. I visited Joe's grave again, several times, and travelled to the gorges south of the Lawn Hill homestead. Goosebumps prickled under my shirt when I stood on those precipices and gazed down steep red cliffs to the mysterious pools below. This was the wilderness Joe was heading for, the place that might have healed him.

I learned more of what had happened to the other players in the Lawn Hill tragedy, how Frank Hann had finally walked off the station he had worked so hard to build, spent years exploring swathes of Western Australia, and ended his days crippled and alone. I learned that Jim Cashman had been stabbed, almost fatally, by one of his own customers at a new hotel in Croydon. Constable Robert Stott, of the Northern Territory Police, went to become Central Australia's first Police Commissioner, and was run over and killed by a train in 1928.

Most touchingly, I learned how Trooper Noble had found God by Lawn Hill Creek on the day of Joe's death. He had walked away from his rifle and uniform and become a stockman for the Doyle brothers. On a droving trip south he reached their property, Invermien, near Scone, New South Wales.

James Doyle, impressed by the earnest young man, offered him a home there, and the one-time police tracker took lessons at Scone Grammar School, entered the seminary, and became the Reverend James

Noble, Australia's first indigenous Anglican minister. He married, moved back to the north, and toiled for the rest of his life for the benefit of his people. By the time of his death he could speak fifteen Indigenous languages.

I spent a week in New Doomadgee in 1968, attending the opening of a hospital. Watching the faces of young men and old women, I had a flash of insight. I understood why Kitty's words had to be recorded. On my return to Sydney I purchased a new ribbon for my typewriter and drew a deep breath.

I had, over the years, travelled much of this country for my work as a linguist, from Wave Hill to Gove, Wilcannia to Palm Island. It dawned on me that there was not just one Joe Flick, but thousands. There was not just one Kitty, but thousands. Not just one Frank Hann, Tom Perry, Jim Cashman or Trooper Noble, but thousands.

Not all are dead. Some of them are still out there now, and their stories are yet to be told.

A selected bibliography of resources used in the preparation of this story is available at:

storiesofoz.com/joeflick

ABOUT THE AUTHOR

As a young adult Greg Barron lived and worked in the Northern Territory and now resides in New South Wales. He enjoys bush travel, offshore and river fishing, reading, writing and long walks. He is the author of a number of books including Whistler's Bones, Red Jack and the Ragged Thirteen, Camp Leichhardt, and Galloping Jones and Other True Stories from Australia's History. All are available in paperback and as eBooks from the usual outlets.